THE VOW
Until Death Do Us Part

Cornelia Smith

Presents
National Bestselling Author
Cornelia Smith

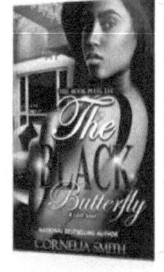

www.thebookplug.com

Table of Contents

PROLOGUE

In front of a crowd full of shoppers, Kimmy takes a tumble for the worse. Her body twirls and jerks as she falls. In the seconds it takes her to reach the ground. she knows it's going to hurt.

She shrieks out, "Ouch," before she even hits the floor. From the check-out counter, comes a high-pitched scream. Kimmy turns her head towards the annoying, bothersome laughter and rolls her eyes. Shoppers could hear the young teens laughing from a mile away, it echoes out Bath and Body Works and into the halls of the mall.

The customers unintentionally pause their shopping, watching as Kimmy scrambles to get up with her things. All eyes are on her, just as planned. She and Alisa were a team. She's king of distractions and diversions, and Alisa is the light-fingered champion. Quickly, Alisa pockets the young girls phone from her pocket and like magic, no one sees anything. Their act is a thing of beauty, it's choreographed to perfection.

Swiftly, Kimmy tosses her purse over her shoulders and dashes out of the store. Trailing just a few steps behind Alisa.

"Did you get it?" Kimmy murmurs.

"Yes, we're good. Now where is that burn out phone I told you to get?" Kimmy scrambles blindly into her purse for about ten seconds.

"Dammit Kimmy, don't tell me you lost the phone"

1

"No, it's in here Ms. Hopkins." Finally, after twenty long seconds, Kimmy pulls the phone out.

"Do you want me to text her from the burn out phone or the iPhone you just got?" Kimmy asks.

"I don't need you to text anyone. I got it from here. You can take the rest of the day off."

"Okay, well I will see you bright and early tomorrow." As soon as Alisa and Kimmy exit the mall, they part ways. Kimmy treks left towards the parked cars and Alisa jumps into the black Escalade that awaits her in front of Westfield Century City Mall.

"Where to Ms. Hopkins?"

"We're going home Ronny," she replies as she texts the unknown number from the burn out phone.

Alisa burn-out phone: You should question the man you with.

Monroe: Who is this?

Alisa burn-out phone: Women like you make it hard for women like me.

Monroe: I don't know what you mean or what you are talking about?

Alisa burn-out phone: How could you call yourself a woman, when you allow your man to cheat on you?

Monroe: I would never tolerate a man cheating on me. I would kill him dead first, but you seem like the chic who would.

Alisa burn-out phone: You should question the man you with, Monroe.

Monroe: Who are you?

Two minutes later: Monroe: Who are you?

Three minutes later: Monroe: Coward!

One minute later: Monroe: How do you know my name?

Twenty seconds later: Monroe: You don't know who you are fucking with. I will fuck you up!

CHAPTER 1

Monroe's frustration builds and she think she might explode - she takes a deep breath, and then exhales. The cool wind from her mouth blows her blonde bang upwards. She wants to shout, have a tantrum, and beat her hands on the stirring wheel like a toddler. She wants to vent, let it out, but she doesn't know who to cuss out, Achton her husband or Dawson her side piece. She pops out a New Port from the packet, smokes it, and takes three more deep breaths before hopping out of the car.

She walks into the resort looking like a model fresh out of a Vogue magazine. Her blonde hair is poker-straight as the California cool breeze blows it backwards, exposing her high cheek bones.

"Reservations for Jan Doe, please," Monroe utters as soon as she reaches the front desk of the hotel.

"Will you be needing a bail boy, Ma'am?" The clerk holds her gaze a split second longer than usual as her brain registers surprise. She tries her best to recollect all the supermodels she knows to make sure Monroe wasn't one of them.

Peoples say that beauty is in the eye of the beholder, but for Monroe that was true of everyone she met. Strangers gazed at her when they thought she was unaware, mesmerized by her exquisiteness.

"No, just the key. That'll be all." Softly, Monroe giggles when she notices the number on the room key-69.

"Enjoy your stay ma'am." The young girl utters before Monroe disappears onto the elevator.

The room is nice, beautiful, and cozy but that's not what's appealing to Monroe. It's the train of clothes—button down t-shirt, boxers, and slacks that trails to the bath room that catches her eye. She quietly strips her body of the curve hugging cocktail dress and makes her way into the restroom. Instantly, Monroe's eyes lock on the sexy silhouette through the fog glass. She opens the door to the shower, and before she can utter a word, Dawson reaches out and grabs her through the steam, and pulls her inside with him.

Dawson lifts her up against the wall, she puts her legs around his waist and he mumbles into her ear, "Damn I miss you, beautiful," before he buries his tongue into her mouth. He's not the best kisser in the world, but as much as Monroe craves him, he could have sucked both of her lips clear off and she wouldn't care. What she loves about him, is how powerful he is. She can feel his big black dick hardened in between her legs. *Black dicks are best*; Monroe believes and she could hardly wait to feel him deep inside of her walls. Monroe's nipples could cut sheetrock they were so hard. Dawson feels them press against his chest. He pulls back a little, just enough to reach down and kiss them.

"Umm, they're so beautiful," he murmurs.

Monroe takes the tip of her tongue and licks straight down the center of his bald head while he bites down gently on her pink hardened pearls. The water is cascading down both of their bodies, and Monroe can feel the head of Dawson's dick rubbing up against her baby-fine pussy hairs. His big body feels so good up against her tiny frame. Achton is a small man, but Dawson outweighs Monroe two to one. His dick is way bigger than Achton's and for that reason and many others Monroe can't leave him alone. She tried once but it didn't work.

"Aaah!" she screams the moment she feels the head of his dick invade her pussy walls.

"Don't run now," he murmurs before pushing his entire dick inside of her.

"I want to hear all that shit you was talking." Dawson's dick is so big; Monroe almost feels paralyzed at first. She tries to get used to the mandingo before she starts to maneuver her pelvic muscles on it.

"Aww, yes baby, yes!" she moans and then starts kissing him deeply while palming his head like a basketball. His dick is so bomb she can't control her hollering. The two are so into each other they never notice Alisa watching through the cracked door. Her blood boils as she watches her husband's porn act. Not only is he cheating on her, but he's cheating on her with a white woman. She slips away from the door, grabs what she came for, and slips right back out of the hotel room. It was if she had never been there.

Meanwhile, Dawson and Monroe continue to fuck each other's brains out.

"Aww, shit girl!" he moans as he shoots a hot load of cum up inside her walls. Monroe thinks their done. They climb out the shower, and Dawson is back at it again. He lays her on cool tile floor and then lifts her legs all the way up in the air, wrapping them around his neck. Monroe can hardly wait for round two. He bangs on her pussy like a drummer. She comes repeatedly. Afterwards, he trails his tongue from her naval to her pussy and then starts his tongue expedition. Monroe can hardly take it. They fuck until they can't anymore and then cuddle up in the bed until Monroe begins her questioning.

"Why don't I come to your house, Mr. Doe?" Dawson was smart enough to keep his name anonymous. To Monroe he is John Doe and to Dawson she is Jane Doe. From the start Monroe was honest with Dawson about being married and the two agreed that night in the bar that they wouldn't reveal their identity to one another.

"You know why you don't come to my house Jane."

"I'm married not you; I don't see the big deal unless you're married too," she nags rubbing his chin beard.

"Nope, I'm not married but you are, with a kid and I don't need no drama," he jumps up from bed and reaches for his boxers.

"What if I said I was ready to give all that up for you, how would you feel?" Gently, Monroe grabs Dawson from behind. His body feels like armor.

"I'll be flattered and then ask you are you sure that's something you want to do?"

"Yes, I'm sure. I can't take not having you in my arms at night anymore. It drives me crazy to be with him when all I want is you," Monroe's words were like music to Dawson, but even your favorite song can get played out.

"I've heard this song a thousand times Monroe and frankly my dear, I'm tired of hearing it. You know how I feel about you, and yet you toy with my emotions for fun. I want you, yes. I would love to marry you one day, yes. But I do not take being played lightly."

In no time, Dawson is fully dressed and heading for the door. Silently, with her mouth drooped open, Monroe watches as her night and shining armor disappears through the door. No more than twenty minutes later, Monroe receives a text from Dawson, so she thinks. In reality it's Alisa texting her through the bluff my call app. *I don't know what is going on, but I just saw your daughter go into this mansion with some grown man. I'm with some potential business partners, so I can't go check it out but here's the address. 3010 Villa Costera Malibu, CA 90265….*

Monroe: *Oh, my fucking goodness! Are you serious?"*

Dawson: *Yes!!!!! Go check it out.*

Monroe: *I'm on the way!*

Dawson: *Be careful.*

Monroe: *I will. Don't worry.*

I love you unconditionally and without hesitation. I Dawson vow to love you, Alisa, encourage you, trust you, and respect you. As a family, we will create a home filled with learning, laughter, and compassion. I promise to work with you to foster and cherish a relationship of equality knowing that together we will build a life far better than either of us could imagine alone. Today, I choose you to be my wife. I accept you as you are, and I offer myself in return. I will care for you, stand beside you, and share with you all of life's adversities and all its joys from this day forward, and all the days of my life.

Tears slowly drip from Alisa's eyes as she watches one of the happiest days of her life on television. Everything was so perfect, the wedding, the vows and the love she and Dawson had for one another.

*I take you as you are, loving who you are now and who you are yet to become. I promise to listen to you and learn from you, to support you and accept your support. I will celebrate your triumphs and mourn your losses as though they were my own. I will love you and have faith in your love for me through all our years and **I will love you until death do us part.***

8

The ending of Alisa's vows repeat in her head like a bad song. She tries to shake the vow and stop her tears but she succeeds at neither. Her tears continue to pour and her vow won't leave her head.

I will love you until death do us part.

I will love you until death do us part.

I will love you until death do us part.

I will love you until death do us part.

I will love you until death do us part.

Like a mad woman, she sits in the dark, with her eyes darting back and forth from the television to the ringing iPhone. Monroe is calling her daughter Chelsey repeatedly but she's getting no answer. Alisa sits and watches the phone ring continually. She can hear Monroe car scurrying up her drive over the wedding video but she doesn't make a move.

"Where is she?" Monroe jumps out of her car and yells. The Gardner looks up to her, confused.

"Who are you looking for ma'am?" he asks.

"I'm looking for my daughter, where is she?" Trained, Monroe pulls her .45 out as she approaches the man and yells again, "Where is she?"

"I don't know who your daughter is ma'am. No kids live here at this estate." Angry, Monroe presses the gun to his temple.

"I will blow your fucking brains out, scatter it all over this pretty little garden." Nervous and confused the gardener pleads for his life, "Please ma'am I'm just the landscaper, I don't know anything." Slowly, Monroe pulls the gun away from his head.

"Don't move!" she yells as she checks her message from Chelsey-*Momma, where are you? I thought you were going to come get me from Dorothy's house?*

Monroe: *Where are you?*

Chelsey: *Momma, OMG! I just told you, I'm at Dorothy's house. That's okay, I'll call dad.*

Monroe: *No. that's fine. I'm on the way. Stay put!*

"Stay put!" Monroe yells at the gardener before swiftly jumping back into her car and scurrying away.

CHAPTER 2

"**M**an your wife sure do spoil you." Old man Paul starts flapping his pink gums as soon as the Lamborghini halts.

"Shut up old man and pump the gas." Dawson jokes before handing him a twenty-dollar bill.

"Where is that fine wife of yours anyway, she hasn't been up here for me to pump her gas all week."

A shower of spit sprinkles onto Dawson's face, he giggles, wipes his face and then replies, "Man do you have to spit on me every time Dawg? And don't worry about my wife. She at work, something your girl don't know anything about."

"What the hell you mean she don't know what work is? She working now!" Paul waves his hand over to his girl who's panhandling on the corner.

"Man, she looks like she begging to me."

"Well got dammit, that means she's working." Dawson burst into laughter.

"We can't all get lucky like you and marry rich."

"I didn't get lucky; I just know how to handle business." Dawson replies.

"You not doing that good with handling business. You haven't given that woman any babies yet. Running around chasing these snow bunnies." Paul murmurs.

"What you talking about old man?"
"Oh don't you mind me; I'm not talking about shit that matters. You tell ole Alisa I said hey, here."

"I'll tell her you asked about her." Dawson responds before firing up his engine.

"Man, that thing sound good." The racing car sits low to the ground and its wheel base is wide for stability. It's a car yet so different to anything you can buy at a local dealer. Engineered to be powerful and designed to offer the least wind resistance. It hugs the turns on the road like the wheels are glued down. As Dawson presses the accelerator he feels all the flesh on his face tug backwards by the g-force.

He takes in the view as he cruises down the coastline. The pomegranate pink sky is beautiful and the weather is perfect. Dawson is feeling like he always feels after a day with Monroe-like a million bucks. That's until he pulls up to the mansion. What is usually a thirty-minute drive, only takes him fifteen-minutes. Hesitantly, he pops out the black Lambo, gaping at his beautiful home that sits beyond the sidewalk, contemplating on if he should go in or not. His energy just wasn't the same when he was home. Alisa's smothering vibes had curse the beautiful mansion.

It didn't matter if she was present or not, her suffocating vibes were always there.

"Shit! Alisa, what are you doing sitting in the dark?" Silently, she wraps up the letter she is writing before responding.

I'm sorry for ruining our marriage, we once had a happy home and I'm determined to get us back to that happy place. We will be happy again, SOON! Don't worry about anything, I got it. It's taken care of.

Love Monroe…..

"How long have you been home? If I knew you were home, I would have brought you something back to eat," Alisa is sitting prim in a black leather desk chair, legs crossed and fingers intertwined over one knee. She snatches off her rubber gloves and tosses them into the trash can beside her desk. She hasn't uttered a word yet but Dawson can feel the confrontation coming. He's keeping himself busy with the dishes he left in the sink, earlier.

"I take you as you are, loving who you are now and who you are yet to become. I promise to listen to you and learn from you, to support you and accept your support. I will celebrate your triumphs and mourn your losses as though they were my own. I will love you and have faith in your love for me through all our years and I will love you until death do us part." Calmly, Alisa recites her vow to Dawson.

"I know love is a gamble and sometimes you win and sometimes, well…...You catch your husband with one of his little snow bunnies. But never, could I have ever prepared for the pain." When Dawson turns at last to face Alisa there is no trace of tears, not in her eyes but there is a web of tears building in the corner of his.

"You know I love you Alisa, we just haven't been happy for a while now." Silently, she watches him put on his best show. Tears are now rolling down his cheeks.

"I gave you everything you have. I made you who you are," Alisa's eyes are narrow, rigid, cold, and hard. In that moment, Dawson realizes he isn't getting to her. Once more he's the enemy.

"Listen, I'm sorry for hurting you Alisa. I love you; I'll always love you." Slowly, Alisa approaches Dawson with her left hand behind her back. Dawson doesn't know what's coming to him. He continues to pour out his heart, "She doesn't mean anything to me. She's just someone who satisfies me while you work. Which is always…."

"I will love you to death do us part," she whispers.

"What?" he blurts. "What you say?" he asks right before she fires the black .45.

"I said, I will love you to death do us part."

CHAPTER 3

Jose bangs on the double doors like they're exclamation marks to his words.

"Ms. Hopkins are you okay?" The sound bounces off the walls inside the house. Repeatedly, he beats down the door, adding terror to Alisa's eardrums for a second time, a third time, and a forth.

"Go away." Three gunshots crack into the air as loud as thunder but without the raw power of a storm. In comparison, they are tiny and small, coming from one direction only-inside of the house. Quickly, Jose takes off hopping like a duck to safety.

Soon after firing the shots, Alisa begins her spring cleaning. Wiping the gun shells clean of her fingerprints with her shirt, burning her clothes in the fire place, and then cleaning her body of any blood. With no plans to run, Alisa patiently waits for the police's arrival.

We have a possible hostage situation at 3010 Villa Costera Malibu, CA 90265.... Dangerously, Monroe U-Turns in the middle of the road.

"That's the same address from earlier," she shrieks out speeding like a bat out of hell to the destination.

"Detective Gosling on the call," Monroe answers into the radio.

"Copy that," dispatch responds. Only ten minutes away, Monroe arrives in good timing. L.A.P. D.'s finest has the mansion surrounded.

"Do we have a hostage negotiator on site?" Monroe questions the first officer to approach her.

"No, actually she is asking for you and only you," the officer responds. Confused, Monroe's left brow rises.

"It's a she, and their asking for me?" she screams trying to speak over the helicopter that is flying over the mansion.

"Now, if you don't want to go in there alone we can send someone in with you."

"Naw, it's best I go alone. I'll be fine," Monroe replies before tacitly approaching the house.

"Ms. Hopkins, it's just me. Officer Gosling, I'm coming in," Alisa watches Monroe on the security camera as she and three officers approach her door. As soon as the first officers push open the cracked door she calmly utters through the intercom.

"Ms. Gosling, trust is very important in situations like these." Startled by the hidden intercom on the porch, all three officers and Monroe jump back two steps.

"Okay, I'm sorry but it would help matters if I wasn't blinded. I need to see what I'm walking into," Monroe replies while waving the officers away.

"Come in, I have no desire to hurt you." Slowly, Monroe peeks her head around the corner and then gradually treks into the seating area with her pistol aimed towards Monroe.

"Is there anyone else here with you Ms. Hopkins?"

"Yes, my husband," Alisa answers.

"Is your husband armed Ms. Hopkins?" Alisa looks over to the kitchen and then back at Monroe and answers, "I don't think so."

"Where is your husband, Ms. Hopkins?"

"He's in the kitchen." Rapidly, Monroe waves her gun around, checking her perimeters. She's so paranoid, Alisa is scarily calm.

"Is he dead?"

"I'm not sure, I believe I might have heard a pulse. Or not," she jokes, with a smirk that mirrors a sociopath.

"How about we both put our guns down, so that we can figure this thing out?" With caution, Monroe kneels to the floor with her gun reached out in front of her. Nervously, she knocks Alisa's written letters off the mantle onto the floor.

"I'm sorry about the mess," Monroe scrambles to pick up the letters and replace them on the mantle. Her gun is still pointed out towards Alisa.

"I'm dropping my gun Ms. Hopkins. I don't want anyone to get hurt. I'm just going to walk over to the kitchen to see if your husband has a pulse, but I'm going to need assurance that you want hurt me," Alisa runs a finger down the .45 with the same expression most women reserve for chocolate.

"Okay, I'll drop my gun but no funny business," she replies before lowering her gun and then sliding it next to Monroe's pistol. Quickly, Monroe slips into the kitchen.

"Oh, my God!" Monroe screams out at the sight of Dawson's body. It looks as if a special effects team has worked over time for some Friday the thirteenth movie set. The blood on his face is thick but not yet dried on his waxy skin.

"What's the matter Ms. Gosling, haven't you seen a body before?" Monroe fights back her tears. She couldn't dare show emotions for a man she has no business knowing. She bends down to check for a pulse and the smell of his bile movement is horrific. It smells like a recently slaughtered animal. Only, in this case the animal is a human and his body is still warm.

"He's got a pulse!" she screams out before quickly running back over to her gun, snatching it up off the floor and then aiming it at Alisa.

"Woah, cow-girl!" Alisa jokes with both hands in the air.

"Did you kill him?"

"Well, apparently not, you just said he has a pulse?"

"Did you shoot him, dammit?" Monroe yells with her gun aimed at Alisa.

"I didn't just shoot him; I shot the shit out of him," she calmly responds with a sinful smirk on her face. There is stillness on both sides. If hatred was visible the air would have been red. Then suddenly movement, so much force in every blow. Monroe rains blows onto Alisa as if she meant to smash her into the very earth. Alisa does nothing. She takes the blows like a child, when being punished by their parents. Monroe didn't just want Alisa dead, she wanted her smashed, obliterated, nothing left to bury.

"Stop it, cut it out. Have you lost your mind?" Detective David questions Monroe as he pulls her off Alisa.

"This is not Jerry Springer. Now read her, her rights. He demands!" Monroe irons the wrinkles out of her clothes, pulls Alisa up from the floor and then places Alisa's hands behind her back.

"Ms. Hopkins, you are under arrest for attempted murder, you have the right to remain silent. Anything you say can and will be used against you in a court of law. You have the right to an attorney. If you cannot afford an attorney, one will be provided for you." Blankly, Alisa gawks Monroe down until she's out of sight. The silly grin on Alisa's face burns Monroe's skin but there is nothing she can do now. It's up to the courts.

CHAPTER 4

Bountiful and proud, Patricia struts into her office with a million-dollar smile and a heart full of joy, not even a bad case will get her down today.

"You have a call on line one, oh and good morning." Her assistant blurts out as she makes her way to her seat.

"Woah, John stop yelling. I agreed to this phone call as a courtesy and now you're trying to take advantage of me." Rooted deep from the south of Texas, Patricia's accent sticks out like a thorn in the streets of California.

"No. I'm not docking it down to a class C. My absence doesn't omit the fact that your client tried to kill her sister-in-law." Relieved from the tiny, burning stilettos, Patricia massages her feet while rocking back and forth at the leather desk chair.

"A gulfing accident, John, your client owns one gulfing club, no balls and the accident happened in a stairwell at a after hour illegal gambling hall. I'll see you in court, well I won't, but someone from this office will." From one phone call to another, Patricia's morning is in full effect.

"Patterson," she answers.

"Hello," Surprise to hear her knew colleague, Patricia jumps up from her seat.

"No I didn't get one. Yeah. Short notice it's fine, it's fine."

Without an invite, Shanell, Patterson supervisor barges in and blurts, "The Hawk—"

Before she can finish her sentence, Patricia quickly silences Shanell with her finger. Impatient, Shanell waits until Patricia is free to yell her frustration.

"Costume, that's fine. What time, that's fine. That's fine, I'll be there. Thank him for me."

"You little sneaky chic, what did you do?" Shanell yells as soon as Patricia ends the call.

"How many times did I just say fine?" Patricia's smile almost never leaves her face and she's looking at Shanell like she's a teenager having a tantrum.

"How the hell did you get a job with *The Hawk* law firm, Patterson? I been here five years, I'm your supervisor. I graduated top of my class—USC, and I haven't been able to land an interview yet. Bite me!" Shanell follows Patricia out to the lobby. Blissfully, Patricia hums, *"You are my sunshine."*

"If you hum, 'You are my sunshine' one more time, I'm going to do something illegal," Shanell jokes.

"So what is all this excitement about?" Nora, Patricia's assistant asks.

"I'm going to need a costume for tonight. Can you find something that can fit these curves in an hour?" Nora nods her head and immediately begins to search the web.

"She's going to need a leash and some knee pads because some ones been doing a lot of ass kissing," Patricia smirks at Shanell's jokes while flipping through her wallet.

"No, not that one, its maxed out. Here try this one."

21

"Will do, oh and God wants to see you." Nora points to the ceiling and says.

"Whose God, our God?" Patricia asks.

"Oh, okay. That's weird," Patricia puns before heading out to see her boss.

"Mr. Koch, Ms. Patterson." The thin brunet announces.

"Come in, have a seat." Mr. Koch says, waving Patricia over to his desk.

"Patricia, no middle initial Patterson. Wow, Ninety-seven percent conviction rates, that's impressive. Of course, you traded all your losing cases to other D. E. A.'s." Mr. Koch flips through Patricia's files, stunned at what he sees.

"Well, I took on two or three cases for everyone I gave away. They just couldn't handle their caseloads and I don't like losing."

"Well you're not going to always win all of your cases over there."

"Working for *The Hawk*, is sort of winning, isn't it?"

"Well, you'll need a middle initial."

"Excuse me sir?" *What bull shit is he up to now,* she thinks.

"All those guys play squash over there and have middle names. They usually go for their mother's maiden name a lot," he witticisms.

"Well, my mother doesn't have a maiden name, sir," Patricia struggles to loosen up. She is fully aware that her boss is trying to crack jokes. It was just never his vibe and adjusting to the new vibe is difficult.

"I'm going to get straight to it. I think you belong here Patterson."

"Well, with all due respect sir, I just didn't work this hard to stay where I don't belong.

"Yeah, I didn't think so. Well, you have your litigation experience, your chops, and um, your UC private sector job. Pretty-soon you'll be sitting courtside at a Lakers game. Is there anything else the city of Los Angeles can do for you?" *Now you're interested in catering to my needs,* Patricia thinks as she remembers the long nights and challenges she had to face just to be seen as an equal here at this office.

"No, that will be all sir," she answers before thinking, *I'm out this bitch,* walking away with a funny smirk on her face. It feels good to have her boss needing and wanting her. She flaunts her smile and struts her curves back to her office where Shanell awaits her with an unwanted gift.

"Congratulations super star." Proudly, Shanell tosses a file into Patricia's lap.

"What is this, Shanell?"

"I don't want to hear you ever say I never looked out for you."

"I just wasted coffee on my clothes and I only have my party gear. I have nothing to wear. Give it to someone else."

"Oh chill Patterson, it's a piece of cake. You got an attempted homicide. A woman tried to kill her husband, he's in a coma. It's not going to trial. There is a weapon with prints and a signed confession. Just go to the arraignment and take the plea. You go in front of Judge Brown at three o'clock."

"Three o' clock? I can't be ready by then," Patricia snaps.

"Well get ready. Technically, you still work here until Monday." Shantell snaps back.

"It's a signed confession?" Patricia questions.

"Spontaneous and signed, now go out with a bang!" Shantell blurts out from the hall.

CHAPTER 5

"**N**ice of you to join us, approachably dressed Ms. Patterson," Patricia smirks at Judge Brown sarcasm.

"I'm sorry about the attire Judge, please forgive me. It's a long story," Patricia takes a pull at her curve hugging little black dress for the second time and then takes her stand at the podium.

"People of the state of California versus Alisa Hopkins."

Finally, Alisa thinks as she rises from the hard bench.

"Your honor, the public defender is representing Ms. Hopkins for her arraignment with the understanding that she will secure private council for all further proceedings." Judge Brown nods and then retorts, "Ms. Hopkins you have been charged with section C664-187 the California penal code for attempted murder. Do you wave further reading of the complaint and complete statement of rights?"

Softly, the public defender whispers to Alisa, "You do."

"I do," Alisa repeats after Ms. White.

"And do you wish to enter a plea at this time?"

"No, but I want to wave my rights to council and represent myself." Judge Brown, Patricia and Ms. White take their attention off their documents and fixate all their attention on Alisa.

"Surely, you won't have trouble finding an attorney, Ms. Hopkins." Judge Brown says, confused.

"No, but I want to do it myself." There is no hesitation in Alisa's tone and that alone is confusing to everyone.

"Your honor, if I can have a moment with my client?" Ms. White quickly blurts out.

"I'm not your client, try to keep up will you." Ms. White is confused, she looks deep into Alisa's empty eyes and surely, she isn't playing.

"You do know this will not be grounds for appeal?"

"Yes, your honor. I know."

"What are you doing?" Ms. White turns to Alisa and questions her, but Alisa fixates her attention on Judge Brown as if Ms. White doesn't exist.

"Ms. Hopkins, you're facing some serious charges here, I strongly advise you to consider legal representation." Judge Brown advise.

"Thank you, but no thanks your honor, I do believe I'm well within my rights."

"Do the people have any objections?"

"Well your honor, we have a verbally and signed confession." Playfully, Alisa tugs at her orange jumpsuit insinuating that Patricia pull her dress back down to her knees. Confused and entertained Patricia pulls her cock-tail dress back down, as close to her knees as she possibly can.

"I will strongly advise Ms. Hopkins to get a competent attorney to try and negotiate a plea."

"That's pretty-jamming evidence, Ms. Hopkins do you want to reconsider?"

"Absolutely not your honor," Alisa answers with a twisted smirk.

"It's going to turn into a circus, your honor," Patricia blurts out.

"I appreciate your concerns of the dignity of the court, Ms. Hot Mama." The court including Patricia burst into laughter in unison at Judge Brown's joke, but Monroe doesn't think anything is funny. She isn't feeling the vibe in the court room and believes Patricia should be doing more.

"Unfortunately, this woman is a tax paying citizen and is entitled by our constitution to try and manipulate the legal system like everyone else," Patricia throws her hand up, signaling no problem.

"If Ms. Hopkins wants to go cold turkey it's going to take a while. Sadly, I won't be here but the people have no objections.

"Your honor—um—I'll like to—um wave my rights to freedom of a hearing and go directly to trial. Will that help you, Ms. Patterson?"

"You don't have to worry about Ms. Patterson Ms. Hopkins, the district attorney will assign another prosecutor."

"No, I like Ms. Patterson."

Judge Brown turns to Patricia and jokes, "Ms. Patterson, she likes you." Again, the court giggles at Judge Brown's humor. Tickled by the craziness, Patricia throws her hands up and joins in on the laughter.

"It appears Ms. Hopkins has a clear understanding of her rights and responsibilities, so it's your call Ms. Patterson."

For a long twenty seconds Patricia stares into Alisa eyes searching for a story; truth, guilt, sadness, anything that warrants her not to take the case. She finds nothing, she couldn't think of one reason not to represent Alisa. So, again she throws her hand in the air, slams her manila folder onto the podium, and answers, "Why not?"

"Oh right then, trial will be move to the first available court date." Closely, Monroe follows Patricia out of the court room to her car.

"Ms. Patterson," she calls out to Patricia before she jumps into the Range Rover. Patricia squints her eyes to get a better view of the nameless face.

"Yes, who's that?"

"It's me Monroe."

Still confused, Patricia wrinkles her face with an annoyed look and replies, "Okay, Monroe, what can I do for you?"

"I'm the lieutenant on this case. I took Hopkins' confession."

"Oh okay, nice to meet you," Patricia extends her hand out to Monroe but she neglects the shake, "Okay then, no shake," Patricia mumbles.

"I hear you're good."

"Good to know," Patricia arrogantly replies.

"Listen are you going to be on this thing because it appears you have one foot out the door already?"

"Well if not, I can assure you, my office will have one of its best on the case," Patricia continues to load her truck with her files, brief case and purse, she neglects stopping to properly talk to Monroe.

"Listen, I don't know what kind of sick games this crazy motha-fucka is playing but I do know she's not dumb. So, I'm going to need you to be on it dammit, and don't throw this case," Monroe doesn't bother waiting on Patricia's response. She struts away, confident that Patricia heard her loud and clear.

"Well damn," Patricia murmurs before driving away.

CHAPTER 6

Walking in the entranceway behind the thin blonde and sexy red head, Patricia feels reluctant to go through with the evening. Had it not been mandatory that employees show, she would have ditched the charity function. She isn't quite ready to be a people person, or to meet new people. It had taken her what seemed like forever to get to know the staff at her current job.

As soon as she is on the elevator, Patricia spins herself around checking out her attire from head to toe in the floor to ceiling mirror.

"Eww, I don't like this dress anymore," she whines and then lets out a heavy sigh. She had felt really-good about the dress when she bought it but like always when she sees it on her body, she concludes she made a mistake. As soon as the doors to the elevator opens, Patricia can hear the mellow, soft sounds of Frankie Beverly and Maze. Nervous, she struts into the dim-lit ball room like a diva on the runway. The important people of California, is dancing, swaying and name-dropping. Not even noticing her entrance.

"Hey, you beautiful young thing." Irritable, Patricia turns to meet to face of the bug-a-boo that had joined her at the bar.

Her mouth drops open when she realizes that the bug-a-boo might not have been a bug-a-boo after all.

"Are you going to save me a dance tonight?" Patricia's hormones increase at the thought of being anywhere close to the dark-chocolate Hershey man. But she knows her heart has a home, so she ignores his question. She then turns her attention to the sound of someone tapping on the microphone and is surprised to see it's Jason; she didn't expect him to be making speeches.

"I want to start by thanking everyone for coming out for *The Hawk* Annual *To Be Blessed* charity ball," Jason begins.

"Every year, we gather here and show our love for the less fortunate. We're not just a law firm who pride themselves on representing some of California's most important and wealthiest citizens, we also pride ourselves on being able to give at least twenty to thirty of California's less fortunate a shot at a fair chance in court, on the house." The room just sounds like money as the tipsy crowd giggles.

"If it weren't for you, and the great benefactors like me we wouldn't be able to keep up this good. So, I thank you." I will also like to think the beautiful Patterson for joining our team." The crowd turns in the direction to the bar were Jason waves his hand. *I'm going to kill 'em*, Patricia thinks as she pastes on a fake smile and wave to the crowd.

"I stole us a lion, yaw can thank me later." The crowd roars with laughter again. Gazing over the well dress crowd, Jason locks eyes with Patricia momentarily and then on Russel. Quickly, he wraps up his speech.

"Now, let us eat, dance, drink and be merry as we all paid two thousand dollars per ticket to do so!"

No later than three seconds after Jason drops the mic, Russel turns to Patricia and says, "So, can I get that dance you promised me?" He asks flashing his beautiful smile.

"Nope, I'm sorry Russel this one here is spoken for." Jason's presence is right on time. Patricia releases a heavy sigh and then retorts, "What took you so long?"

"Aww, baby you know I wasn't going to let no dog bite my baby," he jokes before gawking Russel down with a deadly mug.

"Now, let's get out of here." Tangled in one another's arms, both Patricia and Jason sneak out the nearest exit.

The big black Chevrolet Yukon is parked in the parking lot of the ballroom among the luxury cars and expensive SUV's. It stands out and looks just as good, if not better than the other cars.

"You didn't drive your car, right?" Jason looks over at Patricia and asks before deactivating the alarm on his truck.

"No, you told me not to, so I rode an Uber."

"Oh okay, cool." Jason walks over to the passenger side and opens Patricia's door. After taking her hand and helping her inside, he reaches over and pulls her seat belt into its lock. Giving her a dazzling and satisfying grin he walks over to the driver's side and starts the engine. Opening a case, he grabs a CD and pushes it into the CD changer. The smooth and luscious sound of R Kelly fills the air. Buckling his seat belt, Jason pulls out of the parking lot.

"Oh no you didn't!" Patricia exclaims.

"I didn't what?" Jason asks with concern.

"Oh no you didn't put this on! I can't believe you taking it there tonight."

"Well, I'm trying," he kids.

"Yeah, I see. Keep it up, you might just luck up," Patricia throws her hands up mid-air and smoothly grooves to R Kelly's hit, *Feelin' on your Booty.*

Flipping on the light in the foyer, Patricia leads Jason inside her lavishly decorated town house. She gives herself an imaginary pat on the back for cleaning up earlier out of sheer boredom. Her place is spotless and smells delicious, like the dried citrus peels that she constantly keeps simmering on her stove.

Jason steps into Patricia's domain and instantly, he concludes that Patricia is the one for him. No more contemplating, no more math, no more pro's and con's. *She is perfect, she's the one,* he thinks as he admires her place for the fifth time. He adores Patricia sense of style and her flair of decorating but what he loves most is how she's able to make a house feel like a home. After only six months of dating, Jason is ready for the real deal, he just prays that she is just as ready.

Walking around her spacious living room, Patricia turns on two lamps and then crosses the room to dim the room's main lights.

"I'll be right back with our drinks," Patricia blurts out as she walks into her kitchen.

"Make yourself at home."

"I am at home," Jason replies walking around the room, looking at the new but old pictures on Patricia's mantel.

"I've never seen these photos before!" he yells out.

"No, I change my pictures with the seasons." Jason giggles as he cast his eyes over the beautifully framed snapshots, his eyes stop on a picture that Patricia has taken over her best friend, Jamellah's house the previous Christmas.

Patricia is sprawled out on the floor with Jamellah's baby girl Autumn surrounded by torn Christmas wrap and bows. She and Autumn embraced each other and gave the camera huge smiles. While her smile was perfect and she seemed to have been so happy, he could sense emptiness in her eyes. Not so much emptiness as longing. The longing to be with her own family, in her own house, opening gifts with her own child. The longings that he also has.

Over the six months that Jason's been acquainted with Patricia, he already decided that they would be perfect together. He grew up in an upper-middle-class black household with a genuine, Claire-sassy-like mother and a philandering father. Jason grew to hate the women who called their house night and day, harassing his mother and searching for his father. His mother had been passive, but Jason knew that deep down inside, these things had eaten away at her. Especially, when the secret child popped up.

Although he loves his father, who still lives with his mother in their same spacious Beverly Hills home, he would never forgive him or his whores for hurting his mother. He despises women who made it a habit of trying to break up happy homes and families. His father has since apologized to his mother, whom he showers with expensive cars, clothes, and gifts to make up for the hurt and lost time. His mother, being the wonderful and big-hearted person that she is, accepts her husband's apologies and his newfound love for her. Jason wants all the things that his parents have, minus the hurt and extramarital affairs. And somehow, he knows Patricia can give him these things.

"Here you go," Patricia says as she hands Jason a steaming mug of coffee spiked with Kahlua. She returns with two cups, wearing a soft black satin robe. It pulls tight across her large bust and healthy hips. The view is enough to make the average mind wander.

"Thank you.....The place is spotless; did you clean up because you know I was coming?" he jokes.

"No, Mr. Beachum my place is like this ninety- eight percent of the time. Minus the hours I'm getting dressed," she kids right back.

"Mind if I put on some music?" Jason asks.

"Go right ahead. I can usually tell a lot about a man's mood and what he has on his mind by what music he listens to." Walking towards the entertainment center, Jason begins to look through the scores of CDs, cassettes, and records that are shelved tastefully in alphabetical order. Pulling out a Temptations CD, he places it into the disc changer.

Patricia is not fully aware of his choice until she hears the first few melodic chords of a very familiar song. *I'll be damned*, she thinks. He just put on, *My Girl*. Looking up at him, she notices that he is planted right in front of her.

"We didn't get a chance to dance tonight at the party. Join me." As Patricia blushes, Jason reaches out a hand to her and pulls her up off the couch. He takes her into his scented arms and they begin a slow, seductive rock while *The Temptation's* honey pours out of the speaker. Placing his left hand under her chin, he tilts her face up until they are gazing deep into each other's eyes.

"Who was the guy at the party tonight?" Patricia asks.

"He's a snake and his venom is poisonous. Stay away from him."

"So is he—" moving her face so that she is looking back into his eyes, he cuts her question off and responds to her with the serious expression that he had been wearing when he gave her his first answer.

"Stay away from him." Softly, so softly that Jason almost doesn't hear, Patricia responds.

"I will, Okay. I will." Wrapping her even tighter in his arms, be brings her face up to meet his. Parting her lips with his own, he opens her mouth and tenderly begins to explore it with his tongue. Feeling the slow burn, Patricia responds by returning his passionate kiss. She is completely enthralled by his kiss. Pulling away, Jason looks again into her eyes with his passion-filled ones. Drawing her to him, he continues the fire-starting kiss that they were both caught up in until Patricia's phone rings.

"Aww, shoot. I got to get this. Sorry," she utters before pulling away from his bear hug to grab her phone off the sofa.

"Patterson," she answers.

"The gun doesn't match." David replies.

"What?" Patricia barks.

"We don't have a murder weapon; the gun doesn't match the bullet shells." Heavily Patricia sighs and begins to paste the floor. Nothing is making sense. David sounds hideous.

"The gardener said she never left the house, so the murder weapon is there. Just get your team and go find it, dammit. Shit, it's not rocket science," she snaps before ending the call.

"Why did you take on this case anyway? Give it to someone else who has the time for it." Irritable and crabby that Jason ease dropped on her conversation, Patricia rolls her eyes and replies,

"I tried to give the case away but Shanell wouldn't let me, I can't leave a bad taste in their mouths. I might need them in the future."

"Well you know, losing is not an option. I worked too hard to get you at *The Hawk* and losing a simple case like this could ruin everything." *First off, I scratched your back so you scratched mines. You didn't give me anything,* Patricia wants badly to tell Jason how she feels but she just bites her tongue and replies,

"I'm not going to lose the case don't worry baby." The two dances the rest of the night away and made the night beautiful.

After kissing, laughing, and kissing some more, they cuddle up in each other's arms in front of the fireplace and fall asleep.

CHAPTER 7

*Y*ou betta not cry! Or I'll give you something to cry for. Alisa breaks in a cold sweat as she recalls the horrific weapons from her daddy. Her body jerks as she remembers each blow, she can still feel the pain searing through her skin. Each swipe took away every feeling of safety she ever had. Her father put his all into each strike. His sinewy arm would recoil and snap back to her naked behind, the impact delivered by an object rather than his own hand.

Tears slowly drips from the corner of Alisa glued eyes, which was different because after the first beating, she couldn't remember crying. Crying wasn't allowed. If she buckled he would tell her to stop, or he'd give her something to cry about. He meant it too. Rodger was the first man she'd ever loved, and the first man to break her heart.

As she shifts from one side to another, so does her dream. After Rodger, there was Tony. Alisa's first real boyfriend.

Look at your skin. You black, you ugly, nobody wants to love you. I'm the best thing to ever happen to you. You better think God at night for me, instead of talking that trash. From physical abuse to verbal abuse, Patricia has always gotten the bad end of the stick.

She closes her eyes tighter hoping to stop the horror but instead vivid imagery of her ex-fiancé Charles spitting in her face, appears. An image, that's all it took for the tears to burst Alisa's dam of restraint. She breaks into sobbing; not once opening her eyes. She clutches the solid cold steel bed frame tight in her hand, as she watches the horrific night play out.

Charles: *I want her to be my wife, I love her.*

Alisa: *What about me Charles, I'm your woman.*

Charles: *You're not my woman no more, now let me go dammit!*

It was from that experience, Alisa realized that all men were dogs. She no longer knew how to trust. She was numb, yet somehow in pain. She longs to be free of love, yet she wants to be loved. After the thirty-long minute struggle, Alisa finally opens her eyes. She jumps up from the bed like she had just been bitten by a bed bug.

Dark, empty, cold, the room is a duplicate of Alisa's soul. She jumps from the top bunk, stands, and then wraps her hands around the bars.

"Please Lord, free me of this pain." With a prayer, she pushes with all her might, and after a brief flash of pain, the jail cell itself is mentally pushed to the back of her mind. After being crouched in the dark for so long, she visualizes the light from the sun warming her skin, her black hair flowing in the heavenly wind. She throws her head toward the sky with relief, soon this will be all over and she will never let another get close to her soul again.

"Are you okay?" The soft voice startles Alisa and brings her back to her cold reality.

"Yes, I'm fine."

"No you're not. I heard you crying. I know you're hurting. Having money don't stop the pain," Alisa smirk's arrogantly, as the young girl tries to school her on pain.

"I see you," Alisa sighs irritably and then jumps back onto her top bunk.

"I do. I see pain in those eyes. I can tell it has been there for a life time. I see love too, the love you would be willing to give, if it weren't for the scars. It's still there honey, and one day you'll find a man you can trust to set you free...Free to love again."

"And you know all this why, because ole boy keeps sending you all them letters of lies?" Robin softly runs her fingers over the letters and a soft smile deepens her dimples.

"I'm not perfect, but I know you can never give up on love, because what's a life without it?"

"A peaceful one. A more satisfying one," Alisa answers.

"You don't mean that ma'am, you're just hurt and I'm judging because if you had the guts to kill a man, he must have done something really hurtful to you. Women don't just kill their men," Alisa giggles at that fact. Instantly, she remembers all the pain Dawson's cheating cost her. She's suffered two miscarriages due to stress. She is childless all because her husband can't keep his dick in his pants and honor his vows.

"He's not dead, but he will be," she confidently replies.

"So enough about me love doctor. What are you in for?"

"Being stupid," Robin replies without thought.

"Oh, that's a crime?" Alisa questions with a smirk.

"Apparently, but I found me an angel here on this earth and he's going to help me get out of here. So I can be one with my daughter again."

"Are you talking about this lawyer that you seem to be falling in love with?"

"I'm not falling in love, and yes. I'm talking about my lawyer. I'm so thankful God sent him my way. Lord knows I couldn't afford an attorney of his caliber."

"And you say he's representing you for free?" Alisa confusedly questions.

"Yes, they help a certain number of people every year for free, and I was pulled from the lottery."

"You just be careful and keep your eyes open," Alisa warns her young naïve cell mate.

"Not every man is a bad man Alisa, but I'll keep my eyes open." Robin retorts before rolling back over to catch some Z's before head count.

CHAPTER 8

Patricia has failed at many things in her life but one would never know. Everything from the way she walks, to the way she speaks, to that look of unassailable confidence in her eye says she's the shit, and most noticeably, she's in charge. The crime scene investigators and the officers on the scene begin to scramble—working a little harder than before, when they notice her presence.

"I just thought that umm...Well I don't know, I guess I assumed however it was decorated, it was decorated," Patricia struts into Alisa's house with her phone glued to her ear as usual.

"Well, what do the other junior associates have?" she asks her new assistant.

"Oh, well what's the difference in between the Italian and English?" she whispers, hid in a corner away from detective David and Officer Chin.

"I know they're two different countries, I was speaking in terms of interior design. Can you hold on a second? What design would you say this is?" Patricia steps over to ask David, referring to Alisa's decked out home.

"I don't know, I guess you can call it homicide and modern." David responds with sarcasm, irritated by Patricia's lazy work ethic.

"I don't know, I guess I'll just know it when I see it. Oh, right, bye-bye. I'll see you soon," Patricia snaps right into her work on hand, after ending her call with her assistant about her future work.

"Are you ready to work big shot?" David asks.

"I'm all yours, tell me something good," Patricia follows David over to the gun casing.

"I wish I had something good to tell you. Look at this," David demands pointing to the gun case.

"The case for the .45 found on the scene, now we got no other sign of another gun so far. No weapon, no powder on her hands, no blood on her clothes," Patricia follows David around the house frustrated, pouting like teenagers do when they're aren't getting their way.

"We found three shell casings; .45 is wiped clean, no prints. That's three shots fired, three bullets missing from the case, three shell casings on the floor with no prints on them and a gun that's never been fired. This lady is screwing with us," Patricia's bangs blow upward as she releases cool wind from her mouth, heavily.

"She's stacking the deck." David blurts while Patricia makes herself comfortable on Alisa's five-thousand-dollar sofa, temporarily.

"He's handsome," Patricia utters the moment her eyes lock on the mounted portrait of Dawson and Alisa.

"Look, the gun is in this house," Patricia snaps after jumping back up from the sofa.

"Maybe she was wearing gloves, maybe she had time to change but it's in the house."

"But…" David attempts to respond but Patricia talks right over him.

"And I tell you why I know it's in the house because people were watching the house and she never came out. And I could be wrong but I don't think the gun grew little gun legs and walked out of the house." Short-tempered at Patricia's tone, David sighs heavily, but he knows better to react.

"So if you need more guys, I'm all for it but what I'm not accepting is you not finding me my murder weapon." And just like that, Patricia is done. She waltzes right out of the house the same way she walked in.

CHAPTER 9

The office could take some time getting used to. The view is spectacular. A huge room occupying the corner of the building with floor-to-ceiling windows giving views in two directions. The two remaining walls contained a door, a low bookshelf, and a single oil painting – The old guitarist by Pablo Picasso. The black glass surface of her desk was equally uncluttered: a Mac computer, a leather notebook, and an empty picture frame.

"I guess I'll have to get me a family to put in there," Patricia jokes to her assistant.

"Oh, that shouldn't be a problem," she replies while flipping through important papers for Patricia to sign.

"Be sure to sign the one with the devil in blood, it's not binding otherwise." Jason peeks his head into Patricia's new office and a smile cracks through the creases of her lips.

"I was just going to a meeting, I wanted to stop by and make sure you're getting everything you need." Patricia blushes and responds,

"Oh, I got more than I need."

"I'm running a little late, will you walk with me?" Jason asks Patricia.

"Yeah," Patricia answers before stacking the signed papers onto her desk.

"I'll bring her right back." The assistant waves Jason off.

"Oh no problem, we were just signing papers and talking about furniture," Patricia follows Jason out the door and down the hall.

"More than I need, ugh?" Jason kids.

"Oh, I was just speaking of the furniture," Patricia throws the joke right back at Jason.

"Well don't get too attached, you're not going to be here that much. Two weeks from Tuesday, the whole team is going out to Cleveland."

"Why, what's going on in Cleveland?"

"Sandy Butcher," A light clicks on at the name and Patricia suddenly remembers the case. She snaps her finger and replies, "Oh, the biotech lady who stole three hundred million from her own company?"

"That biotech lady who had no idea what her CFO was doing," Jason corrects Patricia immediately.

"Okay."

"This is a test Patricia, Hawk told me to give you a trial by fire.

"I'm good with a trial by fire," Patricia replies arrogantly.

"He wants you up to speed on eight depositions in two weeks." Jason's speed is increasing and Patricia can barely keep up. The stair case feels like an indoor mountain.

"No problem," Patricia utters between breaths.

"What about your other job?" He turns to ask when they finally reach the top of the stair case.

"Don't worry about it, I got it," Patricia flashes her pearly white teeth and then struts away to the nearest elevator. Jason is amused by her confidence. She wasn't only confident in her work, but in everything she did. He just loves how she thinks the world of herself, even with a plus size figure.

"Patterson," the mail guy yells out as he enters Patricia's office.

"No, no, no. The idea is to get things out of here," Patricia blurts.

"Oh is that the idea," the mail guy jokes as he takes a look around Patricia's cluttered office.

"Yes, and the task gets closer and closer to mission impossible every day." The mail guy grabs a mint as he waits for Patricia to sign for her mail.

"What is this?" Patricia yells.

"I don't know, you're the lawyer," the mail guy jokes.

"Shit, I don't have time for this," Patricia's stress level increases as she flips through the discovery package with the word "No" in big red letters.

"Shit, I don't feel like this, with this damn fool," Patricia murmurs.

"Good luck!" Mr. Post man blurts on his way out the door.

"Yeah right, luck what is that? If I had any, I wouldn't be swamped up to my neck right now," Patricia mumbles.

CHAPTER 10

"**G**uard!" Patricia yells out before entering the soulless gated-room. She strides into the cell like she's walking on gold, popping on her twenty-minute old gum. Aggressively, she slams the discovery package onto the table before joining Alisa. The only noise between the two of them is for a whole thirty seconds as Patricia's popping gum. Silently, she flips through the package while Alisa looks on, entertained at Patricia's arrogance.

"How is my husband?" Alisa breaks the silence and asks.

"I don't know, I'm sure he's been better," Patricia continues to flip through the discovery package refusing to look Alisa in her eyes.

"I heard somewhere that you are supposed to talk to people when they are in a coma. Play their favorite music, it may help get through to them." Unbothered, Patricia mumbles out, "Umm, that's nice of you to do your research," while still signing and flipping through papers.

"But you're probably too busy getting up to speed on the Sandy Butcher case," Alisa's words finally catch Patricia's attention.

For the first time during the visit she picks her head up, sits back in her chair and then locks her eyes on Alisa.

"Excuse me," Patricia blurts staring deep into Alisa sparkling brown eyes.

"Hmm," Alisa mumbles looking back into Patricia's brown eyes.

"Oh don't worry, I'm not judging you Patricia. No, of course not. Anyone coming from where you come from, then paying your way through college all by writing papers for Pristine kids on the internet. My God, sixty-thousand in debt, ninety-seven percent conviction rate. Wow! You deserve it kiddo. I'm proud of you. I know you wish your mother was here to see you excel." Patricia is at a loss for words. In some sick form, she could see herself in Alisa. A strong black, determined woman. It's scary. It's like looking at an unstable twin.

"What have you been doing?" Patricia questions with an entertained smirk on her face.

"Oh, I put in good use of a private investigator."

"Not to investigate me," Patricia blurts.

"Why not, you're investigating me," Alisa snaps back.

"Because you shot your husband." Unconsciously, Patricia scoots to the end of her chair, to be closer to Alisa.

"Allegedly, that's how it works right?" Beyond amused, Patricia scoots back into her chair and giggles. *Oh, I don't even believe this shit*, she thinks chewing even harder on her gum.

"It's kind of hard to introduce evidence in court when it doesn't exist, isn't it?" Noticeably, Patricia is becoming irritable.

"I'm not, I'm not going to play games with you," she stutters.

"I'm afraid you have to kiddo," Alisa's devious smirk boils Patricia's blood quicker than David not having a murder weapon. Smoothly, she turns the channel back to matters on hand.

"What is this, some type of form of communication?" Patricia asks pointing to the discovery.

"Yes, you sent me a box of papers."

"It's called a…." Cantankerous, Patricia takes her gum out and tosses it in the near trash can.

"It's called a discovery," she snaps.

"Okay, that's when the state…" Patricia points her two index fingers towards her breast.

"Is legal obligated to provide all of the evidence to you, the defendant, so you can prepare your defense," Patricia's fingers turns from her chest to Alisa's.

"It's nothing in it Patricia, you haven't really discovered anything." Patricia's right legs shakes like a loose branch on a cold windy day.

"That's one point of view. Another might be that I have hid the mother-load."

"Oh, have they found the gun?" Alisa jokes.

"I don't need the gun to convict you," Patricia barks.

"Hmm, tell me something. Does it bother you that I call you Patricia?"

"No," Patricia answers.

"Patricia, I'll like you to consider becoming my lawyer. I'll pay you lots of money." *Are you kidding me?* Patricia thinks. Sitting in the chair shaking her head in disbelief.

"Alisa, I'm prosecuting you."

"Yes, I know but I'm trying to give you a chance to get on the other side of this unholy mess why you still can."

"Ooh my goodness, are you out of your mind?" Alisa snickers like a kid with something up her sleeves.

"I think under advice of counsel; I'll decline to answer that one."

"Fine, well look, I want to thank you for your offer but I'm going to stay right where I am." Swiftly, Patricia gathers her papers up from the table.

"At least for one more week," Alisa replies with an evil snicker behind it.

"Look, just keep this. Don't send it back. You need that," Patricia slides over the discovery package.

"You also need to come up with a witness list."

"No, I'll leave all that witness crap to you," Alisa snaps waving her hand up at Patricia.

"Right, of course you will. Because you're not going to call any witness, are you?"

"Nope, I'm innocent until proven guilty."

"Right, whatever! You heard the judge; you know that's not grounds for an appeal?" Alisa runs her hands through her kinky-curl fro and blurts, "Aww, sure. I know," Patricia continues to stack the remaining papers into her brief case. The faster she can get away from Alisa the better.

"You know my grandfather was an egg farmer?" Alisa blurts right before Patricia waves her hand for the guard. Slowly, she spins around on her thin heel to face Alisa once more.

"This is not the part when you tell me about your troubled up bringing is it?"

"No of course not. I used to count the eggs for my Papa on his farm. He would tell me to hold them up to a candle light one by one and to look for imperfections. The first time I did it he told me to put all the eggs that was cracked or fraud into a bucket for the bakery. It was three hundred eggs total." Impatient, Patricia waits for the point. Leaning on the chair she was once sitting in. Her heels as usual are killing her feet and she's not sure how much longer she can stand and hear Alisa blab on.

"And umm…he came back two hours later and there were three hundred eggs in the bakery bucket. He asked me, what the hell I was doing? I found a flaw in every single one of them. Moral of the story." *Finally*, Patricia thinks.

"You look close enough, you'll find that everything has a flaw, a weak spot that can break. Sooner or later."

"You looking for mine?" Patricia was no longer impatient but very attentive.

"I already found yours, kiddo."

"What is it?"

"You're a winner, Patricia." Patricia chuckles away her nervousness. She couldn't dare show any signs of weakness.

"Yeah, I guess the jokes on me then. Guard!"

"You can bet your ass on it," Alisa mumbles as she blankly watches Patricia exit.

CHAPTER 11

Patricia steps into the shower and turns the tap until the water becomes scalding hot. Stepping out of the stall briefly, she yanks open a drawer and grabs a rough cotton towel. Getting back under the spray of steaming hot water, she picks up a bar of soap, and along with the towel, proceeds to scrubbing her bountiful body until she thought the dirt had vanished. She soaps and rinse and rinse and soap.

Her mind is loaded and her nervousness is getting the best of her. All night she had Alisa in her thoughts. She doesn't know what to expect today in court and that alone worries her.

"Shit, where is my douche bag?" she questions, looking right in the direction of the douche bag. She fills the douche bag with scalding hot water and rinses herself out like her vagina is the one on trial. Right after douching, she goes back to scratching and scrubbing under every roll on her body. She fears leaving the hot water as it is the only thing keeping her calm.

"She's just toying with you. Pull it together Patricia, you got this," she sings out in the shower.

Hand propped on her hip, Patricia paces back and forth on the court floor twiddling her pencil between her fingers.

"Did you see Ms. Hopkins arrive to the house?"

"Yes," Jose the gardener answers.

"When was that?" Alisa appears to have no interest in the trial, she's instead doodling on a sheet of paper.

"Earlier, maybe four 'o clock." Jose answers.

"Did Ms. Hopkins park in the car pool?"

"No, she always parks in the garage. She's very careful with her cars."

"Would you say Ms. Hopkins is a very careful woman?"

"Ooh yes, always." Jose confidently answers.

"Thank you. No further questions your honor."

"Ms. Hopkins?" Judge Brown utters out to Alisa.

"Oh, hey Jose." Flashing her pearly white teeth, Alisa waves her hand at Jose as if she's happy to see him, and then continues her doodling.

"No Ms. Hopkins, it's your turn to cross examine the witness." Judge Brown retorts.

"Oh, no. No questions," Alisa blurts before fixating her attention back on her art.

"Alright then, Ms. Patterson call your next witness." Judge Brown utters.

"I call officer Smith to the stand." Attentively, the court watches as the officer takes the stand.

"What time did you arrive onto the scene?"

"Five-twelve exactly. We called in SWAT as soon as we knew there was a possible hostage situation. Then I tried to establish contact through the front gate intercom."

"Any answer?" Patricia begins to feel confident again. Her ducks are starting to line up.

"None."

"What then?" The court's attention is distracted from Patricia's question to Alisa tearing a sheet of paper from her composition notebook to ball up.

"I'm sorry, I'm sorry. Please proceed," she whispers out to the court. Officer Smith continues with his answer.

"Two other uniforms arrived. We established perimeters outside the walls as quickly as possible, to keep the house under observation."

"So the house was completely surrounded within minutes of our arrival?" Patricia is feeling herself and finally, she can see this clearly again.

"All four sides."

"And neither of you or any other officers saw anyone go into or come out of that house?"

"No." Officer Smith's answer is perfect and just like that; Patricia is done with him and on to the doctor.

"The bullet pierced through the frontal cortex and temporal lobe; coming to rest on the upper right side of his brain against his skull." Alisa shows no remorse towards the graphics of her husband.

In fact, she's unbothered by the entire trial and it shows in her actions and empty facial expressions.

"Dr. Hill, is it safe to say that someone who inflicted this kind of wound intended to kill?" Irritable, Judge Brown cuts in,

"Ugh, one minute Dr. Hill. Ms. Hopkins, you might want to object. The witness can't know your state of mind." Alisa lifts her head for a split second and responds,

"Oh, no thank you, your honor."

"Fine, proceed Dr. Hill."

"It's safe to say that someone who inflicted that type of wound aimed to kill." Feeling great, Patricia quickly responds,

"Thanks Dr. Hill, that'll be all," she's feeling good and only has one witness left. The witness she knows will rest the case, detective Monroe.

"After you put down your gun, what did Ms. Hopkins do?"

"She confessed to shooting her husband," Patricia throws her hand up at the golden answer and then repeats, "She confessed," as if she had just won the lottery.

"Now did Ms. Hopkins appear confused or impaired in anyway?"

"No," Monroe answers confidently.

"Drunk or on drugs?"

"No, she appeared to be very stable," Monroe answers, looking over at Alisa.

"Detective Monroe, what did Ms. Hopkins say?"

"She said, it was like I just suddenly snapped. I got the gun and I shot my husband, I shot him in the head."

"Objection." The court's attention is now fixated on Alisa. She pulls her glasses from her face and stands to her feet for the first time.

"I'm sorry did something?" Judge Brown asks, clearing his throat.

"I said objection," Alisa repeats.

"On what grounds Ms. Hopkins?" Alisa shrugs her shoulders like a toddler and replies,

"I don't know. Umm, I'm not sure what's the legal terminology, for it."

"Well try to explain it the best way you can."

"Umm, I don't know. Fucking the victim." The court room is instantly out of order. There is chatter everywhere.

"Order, order!" Judge Brown blurts out, banging his gavel.

"Your honor?" Patricia yells out at Judge Brown with her hands waved out waist high.

"You said explain it the best way I can. I'm sorry but what would you call it legally, when the officer that's arresting you is having sexual intercourse with your husband?" Speechless, Monroe shamefully drops her head.

"Now, I think it is cause for an objection. It's rather disgusting, but I don't know what you think? Maybe I'm wrong." The court sits in silence and both Judge Brown and Patricia are confused.

"Umm, Monroe," Alisa calls out for a response but Monroe just shakes her head instead.

"Oh my God," Patricia mumbles under her breath once she notices there is some truth to the accusation.

"Shit," Patricia blurts. Shamefully, Monroe steps down from the stand, and Patricia meets her half way to whisper, "I need to talk to you," Monroe ignores Patricia and struts right past her and to Alisa. Before anyone can see it coming Monroe tackles Alisa backwards out of her chair.

"You mutha-fucka!" Monroe yells out. The mellow chatter is now screams and the Judge is banging his gavel for order. Five to seven minutes later the bailiff gets the court back into order.

"You two in my chambers! Court is in recess!" Judge Brown yells out.

With her scorching eyes, Patricia digs a hole into Alisa soul. Her shaking legs are rattling the table.

"Your honor, she had my witness list she should have filed to suppress."

"I'm sorry, my mistake your honor," Alisa retorts.

"Ms. Hopkins you were warned, you don't get to used that as an excuse to play games in my court room."

"Well, about the fact that it's true?" Alisa's tone increases.

"Ms. Patterson, is this true?" Confused, Patricia throws her hands up and replies,

"I have no idea your honor. I only just heard about five minutes ago."

"Well put her back on the stand if you don't believe me, then."

This is getting out of hand your honor, now she just provoked my witness with an outrageous allegation." Judge Brown takes notes to Patricia's increasing tone, finger pointing, and eye rolling. Indeed, matters were getting out of control. He felt like he was on Jerry Springer, only the two chicks who were fighting is educated.

"My dick has evidence." Both Judge Brown's and Patricia's antennas rise at Alisa's outrageous blurt.

"Excuse me, Ms. Hopkin?"

"My private investigator, I call him dick. He's pretty good too." Seductively, Alisa runs her tongue across her full painted lips as if she's getting ready to eat the dinner of a lifetime.

"Maybe, I should have called him as a witness," Alisa adds.

"Since the tragedy, he's dug up hotel records and witnesses that can confirm my husband and Ms. Monroe was having an affair. My dick is good."

"So what if they were, Judge?"

"Patterson," Judge Brown answers.

"Even if she was," Patricia attempts to make her point but Judge Brown isn't hearing it.

"Patterson, your witness was intimate with a victim and assaulted the defendant." Heavily Patricia sighs and the cool wind from her mouth blows the neat stack of papers off the desk.

"Actually, she also assaulted me why trying to obtain my so-called confession."

"Ah come on!" Patricia blurts.

"It's that a legal argument, ole come on?" Alisa finally had Patricia where she wants her, frustrated, angry—off guard and off her game.

"Don't make me come across this table." The thought of Big Patricia attacking little lean Alisa frightened Judge Brown and instantly, he intervened.

"Listen, no one will be coming across no table in here."

"Geesh, everyone in this court has anger issues," Alisa jokes.

"Your honor, she dictated and signed her confession at the station, long after the incident. Oh, right."

"In fear for my life, since my husband's lover who just had beaten me was in the room with her friends. And the other officers."

"Was Detective Gosling present during Ms. Hopkins' interrogation?" Unsure, Patricia mumbles,

"I don't know, ah-um, maybe."

"If that indeed is the case, the confessions, both of them are out. If Detective Gosling was there during Ms. Hopkins arrest, the confessions and any evidence gathered while Ms. Gosling was present must be excluded as fruit of the poisonous tree."

"Judge Brown, she set all of this up. This is a set-up!"

"I'm sorry Ms. Patterson but I'm not going to allow tampered confessions to fly in my court room."

"With Thanksgiving around the corner, do you think I can go home?" Alisa jokes arrogantly.

"Unbelievable!" Patricia blurts, jumping up from the table.

"Don't push it Ms. Hopkins." Judge Brown snaps.

"What I'm going to do is give Ms. Patterson a few days to come up with some new evidence and if she can't, then maybe you can go home. So, we will reconvene on Monday morning, I think that is all. Thank you," Alisa is entertained, and the twisted smirk on her face indicates she's enjoying the show.

"Well that's final, I'll see you Monday, Kiddo."

"Oh, I don't even believe this shit," Patricia mumbles on her way out.

CHAPTER 12

Sitting still as a mannequin in the dark, Mr. Koch scares the papers right out of Patricia's hands and onto the floor.

"Shit, where did you come from? And why are you sitting in my office in the dark?" Mr. Koch is rocking back and forth in Patricia's leather chair, gawking her down with his dark owl eyes.

"You didn't have the guts to come and talk to me," Koch, breaks his awkward silence and says.

"I was going to, after I figured out how I was going to handle it." Forcefully, Patricia throws her bag into the guess chair and then begins racking up the paper from the floor.

"What makes you think that's your decision?" Koch replies.

"Are you taking me off this case?" Patricia looks up and asks.

"Your bags are already packed."

"It's not over, I can still get a handle on things if I find new evidence."

"From where, the evidence store?" Koch snaps.

"What they open up early a day after Thanksgiving?" It's a completely different feeling being on the losing side and Patricia can hardly get control on her emotions.

"My   witness   lied   to   me,   dammit!"

"Yes, because she could. Because you weren't looking and I know why, because your head is in the fast lane, your focus is somewhere else, on your big salary. And what we do here isn't that important to you anymore."

"Oh, so that's what this is about, isn't it? I'm not going to be like you in twenty years."

"Hey, you be very careful," Koch warns Patricia with his wrinkled finger pointing towards her face.

"You want to judge me, be my guest, but this thing was a set-up. The confession; everything!"

"Maybe, but it didn't have to turn into a public humiliation to this office. You walked in there unprepared, you were arrogant, sloppy, and you did damage. How much damage, we don't even know yet, and I noticed you didn't even care to ask." Koch's words were like hot grits; they are burning Patricia's tongue-leaving her speechless.

"But don't worry your pretty little self-Patricia, we'll clean up after you." Koch's words are final, he stands up, takes a disgusting look at Patricia and then walks away. Beyond angry, Patricia flops into the leather chair, rocking back and forth biting down on her bottom lip. Blankly, she stares out the window, as if a solution would appear to all her problems.

"Hey pretty face." Jason's presence startles Patricia and she almost drops her bags.

"It's me baby, it's me. I'm sorry, I didn't mean to scare you." Jason says after pulling off his helmet.

"What are you doing here, and on that thing?" Patricia blurts.

"I pulled her out just for you."

"What, I'm not getting on no damn motorcycle, Jason. Have you lost your mind?" Jason giggles and then pulls Patricia a Helmet out his bag.

"Come on scary, you'll find it helps relieve stress and you look like you have a lot to relief." For thirty seconds, Patricia stares at the helmet.

"I promise, I got you. Put your bag right here and lets cruise." Charmed by Jason's welcoming smile Patricia grabs the helmet and then hops on the bike. Together, they cruise up the coast on Jason shiny black motorcycle. Patricia is surprisingly enjoying the ride better than she expected. She's always been the girl against fast toys as she believes their just designed for danger but tonight is different. She's enjoying the adrenaline from every fast turn and quick stop.

The two stop for a night at a cozy, secluded bed and breakfast inn. The room is honey-moon ready. It's very romantic with a fireplace and antique Victorian furniture. Beside the sofa is a round little table with a white linen tablecloth and burning white candles. The room also has a huge, king-size bed on a riser with two steps leading up to it.

"Ooh, it's so peaceful here," Patricia blurts before flopping onto the huge down comforter.

"Oh my goodness, who is that?" Patricia shrieks at the sound of the door taps.

"I ordered us dinner," Jason utters out on his way to the door.

"Oh you just have the night all planned out, don't you?" Patricia jokes as she jumps up from the bed to meet Jason midway with the food.

"I figured you needed it, after that fiasco today." And just like that Patricia's mood changes back to frustration.

"Here hold this." Jason hands over the food platter to Patricia while he opens the French doors to the balcony.

"Aah, that breeze feels good," he murmurs as the cool wind enters the room. Patricia joins him on the balcony with the food. She can hardly wait; it's been a long day and she hasn't had a bite to eat. She joins him at the balcony table and the two sip on the Dom Perignon while eating the tender steak, bake potatoes, carrots, and oven-fresh rolls.

"I thought only winners get this treatment," Patricia breaks the silence and says. She knew Jason wasn't going to let the night go without asking about the case. It was only a matter of time before the topic came up, so she breaks the ice

"You'll always be a winner in my book baby but, I am curious to know what happened. How did you let that case slip between your fingers like that?" Slowly, Patricia chops up the food in her mouth, and then answers, "It was a set-up."

"A set-up?" Jason repeats.

"Yes, a set-up, anybody could have easily missed the cracks. Especially, when your witness is lying and keeping things from you," Patricia snaps.

"Calm down, I'm on your side but you got to know, nothing like that can happen again. Not if you're trying to keep your job at *The Hawk*." Jason takes note of Patricia's eye rolling but he's determined to make his point.

"Patricia, I know you're good. I have no doubt about that but good isn't good enough when you are a woman-no scratch that, when you are a black woman trying to get a foot in a white man's door." Like a disobedient teen being schooled by her father Patricia looks away in the sky, while smacking her teeth and rolling her eyes. It's all she can do to stop from crying.

"You have to go 10 times harder than the white man and 5 times harder than the white woman just to be considered equal. Listen, I'm not here to beat you down. I'm just glad that you are off the case, so it won't affect your opportunities at *The Hawk*." In so many words, Jason had just said that he didn't believe that Patricia could win the case and that he was glad she was off it, so she wouldn't look bad. At least that's how she took his words.

After dinner, Jason takes the throw blanket that is sprawled across the sofa and lays it out on the floor by the fireplace. They continue to drink the champagne and toast each other as they watch the embers glisten in the fire and listen to the cool breeze. Seductively, they feed each other's strawberries dipped in chocolate and discuss the motorcycle ride up. Sparks are flying again and for the moment, Patricia isn't thinking about the case. She's horse playing, joking and laughing like a school kid. Jason pulls in closer to Patricia space and the two lock eyes. It's if the world has stopped. Finally, Jason kiss Patricia. He had planned to skip on sex and just make the night beautiful but he couldn't resist. Their tongues intertwine as they begin to kiss deep and passionately. After long minutes of kissing, Jason jumps up from the floor and then picks Patricia up like she only weighed a buck fifty. She wraps her thick legs around his waist as he holds her up against the wall. They begin to kiss again but deeper this time. She caresses the back of his head and runs her fingernails down the center of his back, tickling his spine through his shirt.

He begins to grind his hips between her legs, and she can feel his hard dick applying pressure to her pussy. She then begins to gyrate her hips on top of his dick through his pants. He carries her over to the bed and lets her down gently.

"You're so beautiful," he mumbles while looking into her eyes, stripping his shirt away from his beautiful body. Patricia grips onto the crisp white sheets. Her hormones increase as he kneels before her. This would be the first night he had ever served her, if her assumptions are right. He pulls her pants down her hips and off her body. Next up is her satin green thong bikinis, and off her body they go.

"Do you want it?" he blurts.

"Yes," she moans. Forcefully, Jason flips Patricia onto her stomach and she arches her round ass in the air. He grabs her ass cheeks firmly and bites each one of them softly. Then he suckles on them hard until she grows hickey marks on each one of them. She squirms a little from the pain as he buries his face in between her legs from behind, her ass all in his face. She arches her back, pushing her ass farther towards him. He begins to suck on her clit from behind, her ass all in his face.

He then finger fucks her ass while she grinds her pussy and ass all onto his face and tongue. She moans uncontrollably, he moans right back. After a few minutes of this the two both cums, first Patricia and then Jason. Turns out the night was made beautiful after all because Jason didn't have to penetrate Patricia not once, to feed his crave. A little kiss here and a little kiss there, got the job done.

CHAPTER 13

Patricia knows it's too early to be awake when she notices there is no light struggling to get past the grime of the blinds. She can hear crickets out the window pane as she brings her hand down in a semi-drunken stupor in search of her phone on the night stand. The champagne had done everything but wash her thoughts away. She couldn't get the case out of her head.

"Where you going?" Jason turns over to ask.

"I got to go," she whispers before planting a wet kiss on his cheeks.

"You don't, we have the room for at least five to six more hours," Patricia grabs her gear next to her bed and begins dressing herself.

"I have to go handle some things lover boy," she jokes. To sleepy to fight with Patricia, Jason tucks his face back into the fluffy white pillows and then mumbles out, "Call me when you get home."

"I will," Patricia replies on her way out the door.

"Oh, Patricia. Wait!" Jason jumps up from the bed to catch Patricia at the door.

"Yes," she turns and answers.

"I was wondering if you had something to do on Thanksgiving?" He stutters to ask with his attention wandering everywhere but in Patricia's direction.

"I have to put some face-time in with my family and…"

"Jason, are you asking me to go to your parents' house with you?" Patricia blurts.

"Yes…. Yes, that's it. That's what I was trying to ask. You're so helpful. What would I do without you?" he jokes.

"Yes Jason, I will join you and your family on Thanksgiving," Patricia blushes.

"Thank you, thank you. You, foxy thang you!" Jason shrieks out as he watches Patricia disappear down the hall.

"Patricia Patterson," the mail deliverer meets Patricia at her car as she is exiting.

"Yes."

"I need you to sign here please," Patricia struggles to get out the Uber with her bag and heels in tow.

"What is this?" she mumbles while signing for the package.

"Thank you," she utters, ripping open the box like it's Christmas.

"You gotta be freakin kiddin' me!"

"Fuck!" she yells before throwing the box with the cracked egg inside.

"Ms. Patterson, can I help you. Please, Ms. Patterson can I help you!" The secretary follows Patricia into Mr. Koch's office.

"I want it back," she blurts as soon as the doors opens to his office.

"I take complete responsibility for what happened. Although, I do believe it could have happened to anyone, it wouldn't have happened to me if I was paying attention." Mr. Koch stares blankly into Patricia's brown eyes while chewing the remaining of his tuna salad.

"I'm not giving you back this case so you can repair your ego." Mr. Koch breaks his silence to say.

"Well, it's not just about my ego," Patricia pulls out the available chair and makes herself comfortable.

"It's also about the fact, that…Ugh, this lady…umm, she's enjoying all of this."

"Enjoying this? That's not evidence!" Mr. Koch snaps.

"Right. I know but someone's got to stop her. If you just give me a chance, if there is a way. I'll find it," Patricia leaves her ego out the conversation and pleas for a second chance.

"And if you don't?" Mr. Koch asks. "Listen if you leave now, I replace you. I'm covered, I took some action. But if you go on with this and you lose, I guarantee you, your shiny new job will not be waiting for you. And I keep you on here, this is a public office. It's got a role." The office is awkwardly silent for ten long seconds. Patricia thinks hard and long.

"Do you still want it back?" Mr. Koch ask. After one…two…three…four…five negative thoughts, Patricia murmurs, "Yes."

"Okay." Koch answers before Patricia disappears from the office.

"The gun is in that house," Patricia blurts to David as soon as she struts into her cubicle.

"Yeah, except it's also just not." David snaps back.

"Then what did she do detective, did she tie the mutha-fucka to a got damn helium balloon?" Patricia questions.

"Maybe, I don't know. All I know is, it's not in the house." David flips through his files to avoid eye contact with Patricia. He didn't need to see her eyes to know they were burning a hole through his skin. Patricia takes three deep breaths and then parks her rear into the empty chair at David's desk.

"You know David, your inability to do your job is making it very difficult for me to do mine." Suddenly, she is calm again.

"I'm back in trial Monday," she explains.

"Okay, fine. I'll get a team together. I'll go over there one more time. That's it." David runs his fingers through his oily black hair and rocks back into his chair-proud like he had just saved the day.

"Good, thank you David. You're still my favorite white boy." David giggles at he and Patricia's inside joke, it felt good to have the old Patricia back in business.

CHAPTER 14

Monroe and Achton had been married for more than a decade and Monroe is ready to pack her things up and leave Achton for good. But it isn't because he's a bad man. He isn't physically or emotionally abusive or anything of that nature. It isn't from lack of attention or quality time together either. Monroe has been contemplating about leaving her husband for years because he didn't fuck her right.

When the news came out about her and Dawson, she knew for sure Achton would be ready to pack up his things and their daughter and leave her but she was wrong. Instead, he forgave her, prayed for them and vowed to do better by her, and by her he meant sexually because sex has always been important to Monroe.

Still as a mannequin she lays flat onto her back, suffering through another boring evening. *If this is what he means about doing right by me, I should just leave now.* Monroe thinks as a bead of his sweat drips onto her nose from his forehead.

"Tell me you sorry baby, let me hear you say it!" Usually, Monroe pretended to enjoy Achton sex. Today, she's just not that into acting. Why bother, she figures. It was the same routine, different day. For over ten years, she and her husband made what he thought was love in the dark, in the missionary position, exactly two times a week. While he had his way with her, Monroe's mind drifts to another world. A world where her and Dawson could make out publicly and love each other without limits.

Like clockwork, Achton's nut is gearing up. Three minutes, exactly. *Finally*, she thinks as his body jerks like a stick shift. Her body wrenching in pain but for all the wrong reasons. He had fucked her dry. There is no chemistry, at least not from Monroe's end. As usual, she is pissed and even more horny than before. Monroe never catches her orgasms because Achton is always done before she could ever become aroused enough to come.

"Give me a minute baby, and we can go again." Save by the door bell, Monroe swiftly slips from beneath Achton.

"Let them knock," he murmurs out with his head tucked in the fluffy white pillow.

"It's probably just them damn news anchors." Silently, Monroe shuts the door on Achton. She knew he was probably right but she'd rather talk to the news then suffer through another three minutes with him. Quietly, she peeks out the blinds and to her surprise, it's Patricia at her door steps.

"Shit! fuck!" she mumbles pacing back and forth. It takes Monroe thirty seconds to drum up the courage to open the door.

"To who do I owe this surprise?" Sporting a counterfeit smile, Monroe hopes that the awkwardness that bathes the moment would be transient. She swallows and then inhales heavily.

"To Dawson, I'm assuming," Patricia snaps strutting in without permission. Silently, Monroe exhale's. It's hard to digest defeat. She had easily become the one person she'd worked her whole career trying not to be; unprofessional. As she stands in the door, still trying to drum up more courage to face Patricia, she mean-mugs the paparazzi as the cameras flash and the questions hurdles at her. It's the epitome of embarrassment.

"Ms. Gosling, how does your husband feel about the infidelity?"

"Will you resign Detective Gosling?"

"Did you know your boyfriend was married, Detective Gosling?" The questions boil Monroe's blood. Aggressively, she slams the front door.

"Are you able to talk? Is your daughter here?" Patricia asks.

"My daughter is in the room with my mother and my husband, well, he's updated on everything."

"How long has the media been here?"

"Long enough," Monroe answers.

"What were you thinking to get called to your boyfriend's house?"

"I didn't know it was his house," Patricia flops onto the sofa, sits back and crosses her legs. *This is going to be interesting*; she assumes.

"What was his last name?" Patricia blurts.

"I didn't know his last name," Patricia scoots to the end of the sofa with her ear turned towards Monroe.

"Not his real one anyway." *You gotta be kiddin' me*, Patricia thinks shaking her head in disbelief.

"We met at the Biltmore, same time, twice a week. There were no questions asked and there were no phone calls. Those were the rules; those were his rules," Monroe explains.

"Alright, did you get the feeling he had all these rules because he's done this before with other women?" Patricia and Monroe lock eyes for the first time.

"Be honest," Patricia blurts.

"No. See I don't know if you can understand this because you're a FUCKING LAWYER but this thing that we had, it was real. It wasn't just an affair!" Arrogantly, Patricia chuckles.

"This man.... He made me feel alive." It's clear to Monroe that Patricia can care less about the details to their romance so she stops the explanation and asks, "What was I supposed to do"

"Tell me," Patricia answers.

"I tried," Monroe snaps.

"No, you warned me that she was smart. You didn't tell me that you were dumb," Patricia jumps up from the sofa and grab her things.

"Fuck you, fuck you!" Monroe yells.

"Fuck me? Oh, you already did that," Patricia shrieks back.

"I didn't think that she knew, okay! I just thought the bitch was fucking nuts. Okay? There was no way for me to know that she knew," Monroe follows Patricia to the door with her plea but Patricia is finished with the conversation. She does, and leaves Monroe in suspense of her thoughts and her next move.

CHAPTER 15

T aking a seat at the heavy oak table, Patricia sits her Michael Kors purse in the seat next to her and calls out to Jason as he went into the kitchen to get the food.

"Can't we eat in the kitchen? It's just us and I really don't mind." For three nights, the two of them ate dinner in the large and museum-like room. No matter how simple their meals were, they ate off the best china, and only the finest silverware touched their lips. Patricia feels it's the silliest thing in the world. She wasn't born with a silver spoon in her mouth but Jason was constantly sticking one in her mouth. She'd offer her service in the kitchen ,but Jason turned her down. He said it was the maid's job to cook, not hers.

Although Esperanza is great help and a stellar cook, Patricia wishes she was the woman feeding Jason stomach. She's a black woman, for God's sake! Like so many others, the girl can burn. If their love grows and the two takes it to the next level, she isn't sure she'll be able to allow a Mexican woman to cook for her every night. In fact, she isn't sure about the whole dinner set-up. Some things will have to change, defiantly. She wants to talk and laugh and joke with her future husband at dinner. She wants dinner to be a joyful connecting period of the day, not an event.

Jason seems to be the type who lives out his whole life onstage in front of an audience.

Coming back into the dining room, Jason is carrying the enchiladas, which he had placed on a beautiful glass serving plate.

"Did you hear me, baby? I asked if we could eat in the kitchen for a change," Patricia says.

"I heard you, and I was hoping that my lack of response would be your answer, but I guess it wasn't good enough. Only common people eat in the kitchen, baby. If I wanted to eat in kitchens, I would have rented me an apartment in Compton," he replies, wagging his finger at her like he's the adult and she's the disobedient child.

"I grew up having dinner in a dining room and I don't plan on having it any other way, so you don't have to bother asking me that again."

Biting her tongue, Patricia holds back a flip reply. She remembers the blog post that stated black women couldn't keep a man because of their mouth and she didn't want to lose Jason. Surprisingly, Jason's words hurt Patricia's feelings, she excuses herself to the restroom to wipe her tears. In just a matter of seconds, Jason had shrink Patricia from a feisty plus-sized diva to a vulnerable house wife.

Returning to the dining room, she sits in front of the full plate that Jason had prepared. She's lost her appetite but she manages to take a few bites as she listens to him recount the day's event from the firm. *I wonder if David found a murder weapon yet*, she thinks as her mind wanders from the dinner table. *I know that gun should be in that house somewhere, but where?* She ponders.

Bringing her focus back to her plate of half-eaten enchiladas and Jason's animated conversation, Patricia realizes she's living the life she once dreamt of. Ten years ago, she would have been at her mother's cheap dinette set eating smothered turkey necks and drinking cherry Kool-Aid with a sickening amount of sugar. Now she is sitting at her very successful man's Cherrywood dining room table eating a meal that was prepared by his maid. As she absently laughs at one of Jason's anecdotes about his day, her phone vibrates inside her purse.

"Excuse me baby, I have to take this," she pauses Jason story with one finger.

"Tell me something good David," she answers.

"Well, we tore the whole thing apart. No gun, I'm sorry Patricia," Patricia's ears ring like grenades. Her whole reputation depends on this case and it's easily slipping through her fingers.

"Shit!" she blurts after she ends the call.

"Come on baby, that type of language at the table," Jason retorts.

"I'm sorry baby, I have to go," Patricia jumps up from the table, snatches her purse and then heads for the door.

"But we're in the middle of dinner Patricia." Jason yells out.

"I'm sorry, I got to go Jason. Wrap it up for later," she streaks back on her way out.

"Do you know these two?" Patricia slams the pictures of Dawson and Monroe onto the desk.

"Yes, their two of our regulars," the young clerk at Biltmore hotel answers.

"Yaw have security camera's, right?" Patricia questions.

"Um, yes we do."

"Can I get a copy of the tapes? More specifically, the tape where these two were last seen here at this hotel."

"I'll see what my manager says and I'll get them to you as soon as I can," Patricia heavily exhales.

"See here's the thing, I'm under the gun here. I need those tapes now. I have trial Monday; do you get what I am saying to you." Swiftly, Patricia slips the young girl two crisp hundred dollar bills and in less than twenty minutes, she returns with the tapes.

"Thank you sweet heart, you're a doll," Patricia blurts before strutting out the hotel. Time is ticking and Patricia is determined to win the case; murder weapon or no murder weapon. From the hotel to Alisa's office, Patricia is on a mission.

"Hello, I'm district attorney Patterson and I need to see your boss's office." The chubby Caucasian assistant rolls her eyes and then leads Patricia to Alisa's office.

"Is this exactly the way she left everything or have you moved things around?" Patricia asks as she flips through paper work on Alisa's desk.

"No, I haven't had to come in here since she's been away and yes, this is exactly how she left it. Now if you'll excuse me." The assistant snaps before answering the office phone.

"It's for you. Pick up on line one." Confused, Patricia looks around the office as if the assistant is speaking to someone else, although she and the assistant are the only two in the room.

"Hello," Patricia answers.

"Hey there kiddo, how's it going?" Alisa replies.

"Well, umm-let's see, I'm still out here and you're still in there."

"Yeah, you're right there, pity me. Don't worry, I'll be fine. Is Diana treating you well, I know she can be a Pitbull in a skirt at times. Would you like some coffee, tea maybe?" Amused, Patricia looks at the phone receiver and shakes her head.

"No, I'm good. I don't need Diana drugging me for you," Patricia jokes.

"No of course not, why would I do that?" Tickled, Patricia giggles and continues to shake her head at the amusing Alisa.

"Say, have you found some new evidence, Patricia?" Silence erupts.

What's the matter Patricia we aren't friends anymore? I'm trying to help you. You're in a bad spot and you have nowhere else to turn."

"Okay, I'm going to hang up." Before Patricia can hang up Alisa blurts,

"Will you do me a favor Patricia? Have Diana cancel my husband's tickets. Yeah, we had plans to travel you see, a get-away sort of speak. Next week, actually. Something like a second honey-moon. Painfully ironic that part. I don't think our Dawson is going to make it, do you?" Without warning, Patricia ends the call. Things weren't looking up for her and she couldn't bear to hear Alisa brag about how she's getting away with her husband's murder.

CHAPTER 16

"The power of love brings hope, yet at times the steps toward love cause pain but I choose to gamble on love, as I rather know a life loving you than a life without you. Those who walk towards a life of loneliness are comfortable in their familiarity. But we aren't those individuals. We are born to love and with all necessary courage we will walk the path to it, no matter the roughness, no matter the hardship. Dawson, I will love you hard and I hope you're ready for life with me when you are free. Stay strong, you're only ninety days, thirteen hours, forty-five minutes and twenty seconds away from being here with me."

Nausea swirls uncontrollably in Patricia's empty stomach. Her head swims with half-formed regrets. Her heart for the first time during the case, feels for Alisa. No woman can love a man so hard, with all her heart and then all of sudden, have no love for him at all. Unless, he really did damage to her heart.

"What are you doing?" The nurse startles Patricia and she jumps out of her sorrowful thoughts. Somewhat embarrassed she murmurs,

"I hear if you read something familiar to them, it can help the chances of their recovery. So, I'm reading to him some of the old love letters his wife wrote him when he was incarcerated."

Choosing not to be negative Nancy, the beautiful brunette neglects to tell Patricia that her good efforts were a waste of time. Instead she asks,

"Who told you that?" Beat, Patricia exhales and then answers, "The woman who shot him."

"Are you a member of the family?"

"I'm from the district attorney's office. We—um, we ran out of witnesses," Patricia explains.

"You know he moved earlier." Blankly, Patricia stares at Dawson's lifeless body.

"He moved his eyelids, it's like he was trying to open up his eyes."

"Yeah well sometimes we have to tape their eyes shut. They all move; they flinch, they make sounds. You think they dreaming but they're not, it's just what's left of the system." Smoothly, nurse Betty takes the butter knife from her scrub and gently slide it up the center of Dawson foot.

"Normal reflex is downward, up indicates brain trauma. Even if he comes back, he may not even remember how to speak. Let along who shot him." Patricia's face freezes like nurse Betty had just said a bad word in front of a child.

"What if he can hear you?" she whispers.

"He can't," Nurse Betty whispers back.

"It happens right, people wake up? It's not impossible." Nurse Betty grins at Patricia's hopeful heart.

"What are you going to do? Keep asking the same question different ways to get the answer you want?" Nurse Betty jokes.

"I guess, it's what I do. I'm a lawyer," Patricia answers.

"I knew I should have went to law school." Betty jokes before exiting the room. Leaving Patricia alone with Dawson.

"Well, I'm going to do what I can for you buddy. Pray for me," Patricia mumbles to Dawson.

Patricia swirls the last chitterling around her fork and pops it into her mouth with great relish. It had been so long since she'd eaten them. Too long, in fact, and since she's visiting Jason family for Thanksgiving, she figures she better get full before she stop's by. The family was half vegetarians and half turkey eaters. And she's willing to bet the turkey is the dry chewy type of turkey.

The pork greens, honey baked ham, macaroni and cheese, potato salad and corn bread hit the spot and Patricia was good and full and ready to pretend to love Jason's mother's cooking. Extracting five dollars from her Chanel billfold, Patricia leaves the money on the table as a tip for the doting young waitress, who's the proud owner of a mouthful of gold teeth. Shuddering at the thought of dental gold, she picks up her heavy, matching Chanel bag and walked out the run-down restaurant.

Quickly strutting across the parking lot towards her car, Patricia glances over both her shoulders. She's is acutely afraid of getting mugged, and she is equally afraid of being seen by her girlhood friends, who she avoids at all costs. She was born and raised in Compton and eating at Daddy's Soul Kitchen on Sunday's or during the holiday season was an old tradition.

The run-down hood she'd grown up in, where her older and younger sisters still live, is only two streets away from Daddy's Kitchen. Earlier, she'd had a notion to go and visit, but that was quickly dismissed because she knew that her sisters wouldn't hesitate to ask her for huge loans that they had no intentions on paying back.

Patricia has the urge to enjoy a bit of California's warm Christmas weather, so she decides to take the long way to Jason's parents' house. She drives down Lakeshore Drive, easily navigating the curves. Coming to a deserted spot on the lake, rolling down her windows and sliding back her sunroof, she inhales deeply while glancing out at the serene Lake. December is perfect in California unlike other freezing cities and no matter how many foreign and beautiful places she's traveled to, California will always have her heart.

The squeal of her cell phone breaks her daydream, and she answers it after seeing Jason's number on the caller ID.

"Hey, Big Daddy," she answers playfully.

"Where are you?" Jason asks sharply, ignoring her coyness.

"I just finished up the rest of the packing here at the office, I'm on my way to you now," she lies smoothly.

"You should have called. Try to hurry, we hate to have dinner late," Jason said before disconnecting the call. Patricia holds the dead phone in her hand and lets out a sigh. Sometimes, Jason can be so callous. She contemplates at times whether she wants to continue the relationship or not but when she thinks of his good loving and how he earns his own coins, the confusion instantly disappears.

Popping in a Mariah Carey CD into the drive, she hums along with the songstress and navigates through the traffic on the freeway. When she nears the exit to Jason's parent's house, she rolls her window down and sprays perfume on herself and the interior of the car, which smells like the food she'd been eating only minutes ago. Exiting off the freeway and pulling over into the parking lot of a day-care center, she lifts the Range Rover into park and pull out her make-up bag.

After repairing her Claret lip-stick, which she'd eaten off, and powdering the shine from her skin, she sprays more Rihanna

Crush perfume on her body and in her hair to mask the pungent and clinging smells of soul food until she can take a shower. Satisfied, she pulls out of the lot and continues on her way.

CHAPTER 17

About twenty-minutes after speaking to Jason, Patricia turns onto a palm-tree lined street and drives past the houses of California's black elites. Slowing down as she approaches a large, contemporary home style, she turns into the driveway. Seeing Jason's black Benz parked, she smiles at her earlier decision to pull over and primp up. Parking in the driveway, she presses lock on her car-alarm activator and struts into the house.

The aroma of turkey and steam vegetables meets her as she steps into the dining room where everyone patiently awaits her arrival.

"Hello everyone, I'm sorry I'm late. I got caught up in the office." In unison, the family blurts,

"Hey Patricia."

"Oh, don't worry about it. We all know how that can be," Jason sister Anna adds. Jason stands up to meet Patricia with a wet kiss and then pulls her chair out.

"You smell beautiful," he whispers into her ear.

"Thanks," she replies with a million giggles.

"Would you like some wine?" Anna husband asks Patricia.

"Sure why not," she answers.

"White or dark meat Patricia?" Jason's mother Debbie asks.

"Oh it doesn't matter," she answers. *I'm not going to eat it anyway*, she thinks cracking herself up inside.

"Oh I think Patricia has already chosen the dark side." Jason brother Harold jokes.

"Noo! You're not working with Jason, now are you?" Anna jokes while everyone chimes in with laughter.

"Mr. Harold and little Ms. Anna usually give me a hard time about my firm because unlike their firm we're not afraid to ask for the big bucks." The vibes are easy going and everyone is laughing at everything. Jason's family mirrors those thanksgiving commercials they advertise during the holidays. Deep down, Patricia just wants to laugh at the perfection. Perfect family, perfect turkeys, Claire Huxtable picture-perfect type of mother, the whole nine. The napkins are even folded perfect. The appetizers are dressed fancy and of course the wine is expensive.

"Not always about the money hot shot." Anna jokes.

"No it's not, agree." Jason answers.

"Fine then, surely you want mine if Ms. Patricia donate her great talent to a more noble use, over at the firm." Just kidding, Anna burst into laughter. She couldn't see hot shot Patricia or Jason working for free for nobody.

"You don't have to do this baby, their trying to bring you over to the good side." The corny jokes continue and Patricia decides to take a shot at it since it didn't seem to be going anywhere.

"No it's alright, I get this from time to time and its usually from people who already has money."

"Woah, nice snap back. You win!" Ms. Debbie jokes.

"I usually do," Patricia brags.

"Except in trial this week." Harold adds. The whole table blurts out,

"Ooooh!"

"Nice Harold," Jason replies.

"It's not over until it's over," Patricia arrogantly responds.

"Well, it looked pretty over to me," Anna adds.

"Anyway, Patricia's off the case," Jason retorts.

"It might not seem like it now Patricia but it's really a blessing in disguise." Debbie says before stuffing her mouth with the dry turkey, Patricia assumed they would be having.

"Well, I'm actually not," Patricia responds.

"What?" Jason turns to ask.

"I'm not off the case," Patricia mumbles before digging into the casserole.

"Koch has to do some kind of damage control," Jason blurts.

"Yeah, well. I ask him to let me finish it." Patricia can feel Jason's eyes burning a hole into the left side of her face. She doesn't bother turning to face him because she already knows what his facial expression looks like.

"Unbelievable, you didn't think I would want to know that?" Patricia doesn't bother responding, she just continues to stuff her mouth with the casserole.

"Did you not hear me when I said I had to convince The Hawk not to fire you?" Everyone is awkwardly staring at this point and the tension is so sharp one could cut themselves.

"Can we not do this here?" Patricia murmurs. Jason thinks about his manners and considers waiting for later to continue the conversation. But he couldn't hold out. He couldn't control the built-up frustration.

"I need to talk to you," he snaps before jumping up from the table trooping into the kitchen.

"You lied to me! That doesn't work for me," he shrieks as soon as they are both in the kitchen.

"I didn't lie to you. I told you I can be ready in time and still will be ready in time. I got one thing, one thing I got to do," Patricia replies calmly.

"You're not in yet Patricia, you pulled a stunt and got your foot in the door!" Jason yelled.

"I can still win this case?"

"I don't care Patricia. This is not what this is about!"

"Then what the hell is this about?"

"It's about whether or not you can do what you are told. You wanted corporate right, that was the point?" Silently, Patricia nods her head.

"Did I misunderstand that?"

"No," Patricia mumbles.

"Patricia if you do this, if you win. I'm still strewed, it's says I don't know what my subordinates are doing, my judgements are bad and I'm not in charge of my team. I went out on a limb. I told Koch this was over." Patricia's head drops for ten long seconds, she quietly builds up the courage to reply,

"I didn't ask you to do that Jason." Silently, Debbie watches the argument from the foyer. As soon as Jason storms out, Debbie walks in.

"You know what nobody understands about some low paid public service work. Every now and then, you get to put a fucking steak in a bad guy's heart," Patricia lifts her head up to face Judge Debbie. She wasn't expecting her response at all. *She gets it*, she thinks.

"Now we're not supposed to talk about that when we visit third grade class rooms for career day. And it sure doesn't get you very far in the country club locker room but it's hard to beat when you actually get to do it," Patricia nods in agreement.

"Thank you Judge for that little pick-me-up, now if you'll excuse me. I have some work to do. Thank your family for the lovely evening for me, will you?" Jason's mother nods with a satisfying smirk on her face. And quietly, Patricia sneaks out the back door.

CHAPTER 18

Monroe: *Meet me at the lake*

Patricia: *Why?*

Monroe: *I'll explain when you get here...*

While texting Monroe, Patricia speed walks to her car. She secretly prays Jason doesn't come out and stop her.

*Patricia: I'm on the way...*After keying in her last text, Patricia cranks up the Rover and then speeds out into the road. Easily navigating the curves and swerving in and out of traffic like a pro, Patricia arrives to a deserted spot on the lake in less than fifteen-minutes. Awaiting her with the car lights off, is Monroe. Patricia is appalled by what she sees. Monroe looks like she's aged ten years in ten days. Her hair is a mess and she's picked up at least five pounds. She gets out the Rover and walks over to Monroe's Toyota, curious to why she's here.

"Officer?" Patricia retorts.

"We got to find the gun, Patterson."

"I had three teams out there. Actually..." Before Patricia can finish her sentence, Monroe cuts in and says,

"We know she did it. Right? So, let's find it." Shaking her head *no* slowly, Patricia doesn't like where the conversation is heading. Monroe reaches into her glove department and Patricia's suspicions increase.

"I know a guy in the evidence room. He owes me a favor," Patricia steps away from the car with her hands on her hip. Her head is still shaking in disgust.

"He can swap these with the shells in evidence and give us a ballistics match and we'll have our gun," Monroe waves around the .45 bullets in the zip lock bag. Patricia listens to Monroe until she can't take it anymore. She hates having the opportunity to do the wrong thing. She hates Monroe even more for putting her between a rock and hard place.

"Go home, Monroe." Patricia leans into the car and says. Monroe reeks of booze. The smell is so strong it brings water to Patricia's eyes.

"Go home and get off the streets before you kill somebody," Patricia walks away without warning.

"What else you got, hot shot? What else do you have, Patterson?" Monroe screams at Patricia. Making a right turn out of the parking lot, Patricia heads south to I-10 East to Riverside condo. She hums along to Mariah Carey trying to sing away her heavy thoughts. When she nears the exit to her house, she's drowning with sorrow. She didn't feel like being along but she didn't want to be with Jason either. Her emotions are flying high and getting the best of her.

The clear and opal bubbles hiss and makes soft swishing sounds as they burst around Patricia's thick thighs. The once steaming water has turned warm and a chill is beginning to take over her body. Reaching over, she pulls the tub plug and let out some of the water. Turning on the hot-water tap, she refills the tub with hot water. Squeezing more foam into the water, she settles back and closes her eyes.

Hearing her phone ring, she isn't ready to get out of the tub and face the life that she now calls her own. Everything that she always wanted was now hers, but she still can't decide whether or not she is satisfied with it. She has a good man, who has potential to be her husband. He pleases her physically and financially. A career she adores, and all the material things she can possibly want. But, at times like today, she still feels a certain emptiness that she cannot explain. Maybe, it's because she hasn't experienced much of life due to working so hard. Or maybe it's because she had such a distant relationship with her family. Or it could possibly be something she hadn't discovered yet.

Whatever it is, it creeps up on her every so often and makes her feel like a motherless child. Patricia feels the warm and salty tears slide down her face but cannot explain their presence. The two initial tears soon turn into a rainstorm of weeping that she can't control. Feeling that she is no longer in control of herself, she begins bawling as she hadn't for years.

Boom, clack!

Finally, the book she had been meaning to pull back from the edge of the sofa had just hit the floor. Patricia stops her crying and looks at the bathroom door as if she could see the book hit the floor through the door. Dismissing the distraction, she abruptly goes back into bawling.

Coming out the bathroom wrapped in her white cotton robe, Patricia sits on the edge of the bed. Releasing the robe from her ample body she begins to smear on Palmer's Cocoa Butter, a staple from her girl hood. Enjoying the smell and smooth feeling of the lotion, her spirits instantly lift. Finally, she's emotionally stable enough to listen to Jason's voicemail. She key's in her password, put the phone on speaker and then lays it flat onto her bed.

Hey, it's me. Things sort of got out of hand today and I guess…. Well I guess neither one of us was expecting drama in our lives right now. And I think we have to…… I think we have to figure out what to do about that. This is where to find me, call me. Patricia squeezes more lotion into her hands and rubs it onto her smooth arms. Satisfied with the results, she snaps the bottle closed. She didn't give what Jason said a second thought. To her he wasn't speaking about anything. Nothing she had wanted to hear. An apology for his behavior would have been nice or a pick me up joke about the disagreement would have even been accepted but no, all he did was ramble about nothing. Over Jason, she clicks to the next message.

Hey Ms. Patterson, this is Stephanie from the Biltmore hotel. Apparently, there was a screw-up in the tapes I gave you. I have the tape for the date you requested here. If it's not too late, you can come get them as soon as tomorrow morning.

"Great," Patricia mumbles as she presses three on the key pad to save the message. Kneeling at the edge of her bed, Patricia says a quick prayer and then slides under the starched cotton sheets sprinkled with Johnson and Johnson baby powder. Most of Patricia's new friends thought this idea was super ghetto but she didn't care. She needed it to sleep. It's the only ghetto ritual she took with her out the hood.

CHAPTER 19

"**G**ood news," David says as soon as Patricia takes a seat at his desk.

"Thanks for picking up the tape. I over slept and the young girl's shift was ending, so I wasn't going to make it in time," Patricia breathlessly explains. Smiling at his co-worker's apology, David notices for the thousandth time how cute Patricia is. Although most men would consider Patricia fat, David feels she is perfect. She's about five feet eight and weighs well over two hundred pounds, but she carries her weight like she is less than a hundred. Her warm chocolate face is smooth, with full lips, high cheek bones, and slanted hazel eyes. Braces that her mother could not afford to give her when she was a young girl now adorn her teeth an only add to her cuteness.

Along with social status, Patricia has gained a terrific sense of style. Essence, Elle, and Ebony were fashion bibles and everything she wears complements her large chest and heavy hips. She's blossomed from a dumpy fat girl into a well-dressed plus-size woman.

"It wasn't a problem; I wasn't too far from the hotel," David responds.

"Oh hell, why were you in the area? You don't have a side piece whose name you don't know, too, do you?" David giggles at Patricia's joke while popping in the tape.

"Of course not my love. I wouldn't dream of cheating on you," he jokes before getting back to business.

"Check this out, we got her," David blurts as Alisa enters the hotel. Irritable, Patricia exhales. The cool air from her mouth blows the stack of papers tucked beneath the stapler upward.

"I thought you had me something David," she finally responds after taking three deep breaths.

"I do, we got her right here on tape. We got her at the hotel on the day of the murder." Recurrently, Patricia shakes her head *no*.

"You know it's her, it's no doubt that the woman is her," David explains.

"Well, there's no face," Patricia replies staring blankly at the video.

"So we enhance it." David snaps.

"Enhance what, a hat?" Patricia snaps back.

"We know it's her, she's there on the day she shot him."

"And why is she there?" The ball point pen slips from Patricia fingers onto the desk.

"And why is she there, the day of?" Patricia asks David again before jumping up from her seat.

"What are you talking about?" David questions, looking at Patricia as if she is a crossword puzzle with no possible solution.

"This is a woman who plans everything down to the hat, okay. What is she doing there the day of? What part of the plan is that?" Patricia shouts.

"She's there because she has to see it for herself." David yells back.

"They're at the room, she didn't barge in because they would have known she was there. So why did she go to the room?" Frustrated, Patricia tosses her briefcase across the room.

"Yeah, they're at the room. She's jealous, her husband is having an affair." Repeatedly, Patricia screams, "No, no, no!"

"Come on, she's there. She's getting worked up, she's planning to shoot him. This woman, this woman here, she's sick. And the point you're missing here, is we just caught this senseless woman on tape." David blurts, jumping up from his seat for the second time.

"We have motive," David adds.

"We have motive," Patricia repeats with a giggle.

"I don't have motive! I don't have motive unless I have him and I don't have face, so I don't have him."

"That is such lawyer, bullshit!" Green veins swivel around David's forehead.

"It is lawyer shit, why you think I'm getting out of criminal law!" The two dart back and forth with their words like a real married couple.

"I'll tell you something else, I'm not going to end my career on a case where all I have is an enhance hat. When what I should have is a murder weapon and what—"

"Aah, come on. That is new evidence!" David cuts in and yells.

"I should have a signed confession!" At this point, they aren't talking to each other but instead yelling at each other.

"I told you from day one, that she is playing games but you had your got-damn head so into your new work, you weren't paying attention!"

"You're the one who couldn't find my gun and you're the one who let Monroe take a confession from a woman she had just beaten up."

"Monroe lied to me, dammit! That wasn't my fault."

"Whatever," Patricia takes a deep breath and mumbles.

"If you'll excuse me, I got to go make a case out of nothing." Swiftly, Patricia snatches up her brief case and prances out the door.

"You're just being an ass-whole in heels as usual." David blurts at her as she struts out the office.

Patricia is in dying need of a miracle. She feels as if she's weakened and she needs something to light the fire back inside her. So, she visits her old stomping grounds. Seeing where she came from is always motivation. Just the thought of having to return lit the dim fire in her but she didn't need a little camp fire, but a wild fire to take Alisa down. So, she did more than drive around the hood, she actually stopped by her sister's house.

Walking up the seedy sidewalk, Patricia feels like she is walking to her own execution. Looking over her shoulder to make sure her Range Rover is still there; she turns back around and knocks on the torn screen door. Through the greasy glass, she can see the unkempt living room where she had learned to walk, talk, and think. She can feel that familiar feeling in the pit of her stomach.

Okay, Patricia. Just remember, you're only here to visit. You'll be leaving here in a few minutes. You don't live here anymore. She thinks. Looking up she sees her younger sister wiggling to the door. Tonya no longer looks like Patricia's younger sister. She now looks like a fat and run-down version of Patricia. Childbirth and constant partying has taken their toll on her once good looks. Now, looking at Patricia is no longer like looking in the mirror. It's more like peering in one of the catalogs that had served as wish-books for them when they were young girls.

"Girl you know you don't have to knock when you come here!" Tonya exclaimed loudly.

"Where the bags at? What you bought me?" Hating to disappoint her sister, Patricia made speedy promises to clean out her closet and bring Tonya all the things that no longer fit.

Walking into the door that Tonya holds open for her, she is greeted by damp darkness and the smell of day-old chicken grease.

Half listening to Tonya's story about a dope boy who had taken her to get her hair done two weeks earlier, Pat is once again reminded of why she hated to visit. Her older sister, all gold teeth and gold hair, soon comes into the dank living room to greet her *rich little sister*, as she often refers to Pat. Proud of her little sister's new status, she still dreams and have faith that her and Tonya will to find their prince charming, who will sweep them away from the ghetto.

For an hour, Patricia sits listening to her sisters complain, prod, and beg. When she knew she could not take anymore, she opens her purse and writes two checks: one for Tonya and one for Sophia. Handing the checks to them, she is instantly disgusted when their complaints are replaced by fake inquiries about her work and social life. Growing more disgusted by the minute, she gathers up her purse and makes a hasty excuse to leave, taking her full her heart with her.

Jumping back into her Rover and driving down the freeway, she let the tears flow. Why can't she have a family who is happy with her success instead of in love with it? As the tears collect under her chin, she notices that she got what she needed to sock it to Alisa tomorrow in court.

CHAPTER 20

The squeal of the cell phone breaks Patricia's sleep. Blindly, she waves her hand over to the night stand to grab her phone.

"Hello," she whispers.

"It's done. In the restroom, stall three taped beneath the toilet," Monroe ends the call as soon as she finishes talking.

"Fuck!" Patricia screams when she finally opens her eyes and look around her bedroom. A wave of fear paralyzes her and she can't move. Her heart is racing, as if she's been running. Her forehead is wet and so are her pajamas. It's not from night sweats. It's the case, Alisa has her tripping like never before. Her hands are tingling but she can't shake them. Not yet. She can blink, which she does until she's batting her eyes; anything to send the fear of losing away, to the back of her mind. She usually doesn't get nervous before court but when she does, it gives her anxiety. Occasionally, anxiety shows up and jumps inside her. When it does, she waits the five or ten minutes it takes for her breathing to slow down and then she can feel the blood flowing into her fingertips, again.

Right now, the sun is peeking through the space between the shutters. Patricia knows she needs to get her act together because court is approaching in a couple of hours.

She counts to three, rolls on her side and opens the drawer to the table. She reaches for two prescription bottles, swallows the Xanax dry. She doesn't know why she even bothers taking them because they do nothing for her. Maybe taking them makes her feel like she's on the verge to normal again. She's confused on how women get so addicted to them because feeling spaced out was something she didn't want to feel every day.

Patricia speed dialed her old assistant and demands she meet her at The Old Bistro below their office. Wasting no time, Patricia takes a shower, washes her face, brushes her teeth, and slips on the most striking court suit she owns. In less than ten minutes, Patricia is sitting at a table in The Old Bistro waiting for Mona. She's a half hour late. Patricia wants to call but figures she's just panicking from paranoia.

Patricia is staring out the window at the heat waves wiggling. At the giant sun. The cloudless sky. The breeze is so hot you don't want to inhale.

"Are you almost ready to order?" The waitress asks as she freshens Patricia's coffee.

"Just give me a few more minutes. Thanks." When Patricia spots Mona heading for her table she's instantly nervous all over again. She only knew how to play by the rules, which was crazy because she's probably the only DA in her office that's from the hood.

"Hey, sorry I'm late," Patricia stands up and gives Mona a hug.

"You smell good," Patricia is starting to act like a man who wanted something from a lady. The compliments always come first.

"Oh thank you," Mona replies.

"I'm starving. What are you having?" Mona asks.

"Maybe an omelet."

"I'll take some banana pancakes and bacon," Mona says.

The waitress brings more coffee and takes their order. They are quiet for a few minutes. They look out the window, then at each other.

"So what's going on, Patricia?" Blankly, Patricia stares back out the window for another some odd minutes, contemplating if she should bring Mona into the shenanigans or not.

"Did I do something wrong?" Mona interrupts the awkward silence to ask.

"No, of course not. I'm not mad at you. I'm just thinking, that's all."

"Oh, okay. Are you alright?" Patricia sighs heavily. Then giggles but she never answers Mona's question.

"Can I ask you to do something for me this morning?" Slowly, Mona nods her head.

"Do you have your cell phone on you?" Patricia asks.

"Yeah, of course."

"Could you sit outside the courtroom because I might call you. And if I do, just hang up and come inside and whisper something in my ear about finding the murder weapon." Mona's smile reaches from one ear to another.

"You found the murder weapon?" she nods with a satisfying grin on her face.

"I haven't decided that yet," Patricia replies.

"Okay," she responds confused.

The courthouse is a circus, camera flashing, reporters yelling; the whole nine. Nervous, Patricia struts through the crowd like she has her shit together, when reality is, she has no game plan. She's literally walking into a lion pit clothed in meat. On her way into the courtroom she spots Monroe in the back of the crowd. The two lock eyes momentarily and then Monroe disappears through the crowd.

"Order in the court." Robotically, the court comes to attention at the sound of the banging gavel.

"Ms. Patterson," Judge Brown calls out as she flips through paper work.

"Um, your honor?" Alisa blurts out. "I will like to submit a motion at this time." With a puzzled face, Patricia turns to face Alisa.

"What type of motion Ms. Hopkins?" Judge Brown asks.

"I rule for a judgement of acquittal," Alisa replies.

"Objection!" Patricia blurts.

"On what grounds?" Judge Brown asks Alisa.

"Well the prosecutor doesn't have any actual evidence proving that I did anything."

"But, I'm about to present my evidence your honor," Patricia's tone loses an octave as she retorts the lie.

"And all of her witnesses will testify to the same facts that—um...That my husband was shot and that I was tragically in the house at the time of the incident. And in a way, a victim myself. I went over the testimony of Ms. Patterson's entire witness list myself and according to California I should move for…. A… what's the legal terminology for it…" Alisa pulls out a paper from her folder but she doesn't actually read it to finish her sentence. Instead she just waves the paper around as she speaks.

"California penal code section 118.1 for judgement of acquittal on the grounds of the evidence presented before this court is insufficient to sustain a conviction. Thank you," she finishes in a speedy matter, not stopping once to breathe between words.

"Your legal skills seem to have improved over the long weekend, Ms. Hopkins."

"Ms. Patterson, do you have any new evidence?" The entire court's attention turns to Patricia as if they're being hypnotized following the dangling rope.

"Your honor, can I have a moment?" Butterflies swim freely in the pit of Patricia's guts. She's confused. She sits in her chair and pops out her cell phone, scrolling down her contacts. *Should I call her or not*, she thinks as the court-room waits in suspense.

"Um, your honor?" Alisa blurts out.

"Ms. Patterson?" Judge Brown calls out. And the court room is quiet for twenty more awkward seconds.

Tears can drip from Patricia's eyes if she blinks, that's how upsetting the moment is for her. *Shit*, she thinks as she debates back and forth with her good and evil. Meanwhile, Mona is sitting outside the court sweating bullets, waiting on a call of action.

"Ms. Patterson," Judge Brown speaks out before Patricia jumps up from her seat to say, "I have no further evidence at this time your honor."

Monroe is appalled, she badly wants to jump over the gate that's between her and Patricia and just choke the life out of her but she knew another episode like the last one would wind her up in jail this time.

Patricia's nervous system feels as though it's going to shut down as she listens to the small chatter behind her. The court is filled with important people's including her boss Koch.

"Motion for a judgement of acquittal is granted." Judge Brown murmurs with disappointment.

"The jury is released with our apologies and the defendant is free to go," Alisa squeezes her eyes tight and mumbles, "Yes," at the sound of the gavel banging.

"Thank you, your honor. Thank you." The court slowly empties out but Patricia stays glued to her chair. Embarrassment is an understatement.

"Even a broken clock, gets it right twice a day," Alisa murmurs to Patricia on her way out.

CHAPTER 21

The squeal of Patricia cell phone breaks her reverie. She scrambles blindly through her purse for the phone. She doesn't bother saying hello, she simply holds the phone to her ear.

"Patricia, hey. I just heard. I'm sorry." Jason hears Patricia breathing through the phone but she doesn't speak.

"What you think I wasn't keeping tabs?" he jokes but she isn't laughing.

"I don't know what I thought," she mumbles sadly.

"Listen, what do you say, I take you out tonight and we get completely trashed." Before Patricia can respond a loud *Boom*, similar to a stadium fire work goes off. Quickly, without second thought, Patricia jumps up from the table and runs out the court room to the hall towards the noise.

"Patricia, what's that? Are you okay? What happened?" Jason screams through the phone but there is no answer. Patricia and other civilians of the court are running towards the noise.

"Oh, wow! You got to be kiddin' me?" Patricia murmurs as she blankly stares at Monroe's lifeless body. Her blood and brain are scattered all over the court walls. One visible bullet wound one blow to the head.

BREAKING NEWS-"We are standing in front of the court of Los Angeles where detective Monroe Gosling, has just taken her life. It appears the court verdict was too much for her to handle. The story and details are still developing but we will keep you updated here on Fox Eleven Los Angeles live." Meanwhile, Achton stares emptily at the television, he and Chelsey had watched the news to hear the verdict but never did they expect to hear Monroe wouldn't be returning home.

I love you unconditionally and without hesitation. I Dawson vow to love you, Alisa, encourage you, trust you, and respect you. As a family, we will create a home filled with learning, laughter, and compassion. I promise to work with you to foster and cherish a relationship of equality knowing that together we will build a life far better than either of us could imagine alone. Today, I choose you to be my wife. I accept you as you are, and I offer myself in return. I will care for you, stand beside you, and share with you all of life's adversities and all its joys from this day forward, and all the days of my life.

For the thousandth time, Alisa watches her wedding video. Tears slowly drips from her eyes as she remembers the beautiful moment. Alisa and Dawson had a breathtakingly beautiful wedding at Saint Benedict the Moor Cathedral and a lavish reception at a prestigious ballroom. Dawson's mother and step sister had spread the word about the location, time, and date of the wedding to half of Compton. Alisa watched, at first, in disturbed horror as a large number of Dawson's old acquaintances and neighbors marched into the reception and took over as if it were a house party. But when Dawson's mother got done demonstrating her skills in doing the Electric Slide, Alisa was alright again. Dawson's mother wore her special mother-of-the-groom outfit that she had purchased from Chong Lee's Beauty Supplies and Fashion. The bright pink dress overlaid with white lace contrasted starkly with the baby pink pearl-studded stockings and hot pink vinyl pumps. She looked a mess but Dawson wasn't ashamed of her, not one bit. If anyone had told her that she didn't look good, they would have had to deal with Dawson. He loved his mother, she was his rock but after she overdosed Dawson changed.

Alisa mourned Gloria's death after the fact. She wasn't too sad about her leaving until she noticed Gloria was the one keeping Dawson in line when it came to him treating her with respect. Gloria herself had her bad run-ins with men and she made sure her son wasn't out doing to women what his father had done to her.

The clear opal suds hiss and make soft whooshing noises as they burst around Alisa's petite thighs. She's been in the tub for hours trying to wipe her body clean of the jail germs. The once sweltering hot water has turned tepid and a chill is beginning to take over her body. Reaching over, she pulls the tub pad and lets out some of the water. Turning on the hot-water tap, she refills the tub with hot water. Squeezing more bubbles into the water, she settles back and closes her eyes. Her favorite part of the wedding is playing. She reaches her dripping hand out the water to grab the remote that is close by on the floor to turn up the TV that's mounted on a wall in front of the tub.

A *Ribbon in The Sky*, by Stevie Wonder is playing and she and Dawson are wrapped into each other's arms, dancing the night away. It was perfect. Their love felt like the real thing and every time she is reminded that it wasn't, she gets angry all over again. Alisa feels a warm and briny tear drop down her face, she knows she's due for a good cry but she just doesn't want to. She hated to give Dawson, her father, or any other man another tear. She's tired of being the broken-hearted girl and for once she just wants to be genuinely happy. She wants them, the men who hurt her, to be the bitter-angry-salty ones.

The two initial tears turn into a rainstorm of weeping that she cannot control. Feeling that she is no longer in control of herself, she begins to cry. Really cry, not shed a few tears cry but, she bawls with long pauses in between her whimpers. If someone could hear Alisa, they would think someone was trying to kill her but no one was home. Yet, again she is all alone. Alisa has been scared of lonely since she lost her family back home in South Africa. And now because of Dawson, she must start all over. She's forced to face her fears alone, all over again.

When the water is cold again, Alisa gets out the tub, lotions her body and pops a Xanax before tucking herself deep under her covers. She tries her hardest to block out the frightening silence. She would turn the TV on but the sound of infomercials bores her, and strangely keeps her up at the same time. She would lift her eyelids to see the item they were selling even if she wasn't interested. After another long hour of weeping, she finally doses off to sleep.

CHAPTER 22

"I'm sorry, I failed you miserably today. I let her slip through my hands. I just wouldn't be able to live with myself if I didn't get her by the book. Plus, I had a strange feeling somehow, she would have made me regret that choice. We need you now, you're our only hope. I need you to fight; fight for your life, so you can fight for justice."

Nurse Betty stands silently in the door, watching in on Patricia talk to Dawson. It's clear, Patricia is emotionally involved with the case. Her eyes are wet, her hand trembles as she rubs Dawson, and her voice is cracking as she speaks. For hours, Patricia speaks to Dawson. Reading him books, playing his favorite music silently on her phone.

The sun's beams creep through the blinds and shine on Patricia and Dawson's faces.

"Ms. Patterson, what a pleasant surprise." The sound of Alisa's voice wakes a sleeping Patricia, and she opens her eyes. She can't believe her ears. She's surprised to see Alisa at the hospital, until she remembers Alisa is a free woman and she and Dawson are still very much married.

"Don't tell me let, me guess. You've gotten religious on me, haven't you? You've found God and all that good stuff. It's not just the winning and the losing anymore, it's the injustice of it, right?" Swiftly, Patricia scoops up her bag and then she throws her jacket on. The quicker she can get out of the room with Alisa the better. She's not sure how long she can ignore Alisa's bragging.

"This is priceless," Alisa giggles as she follows Patricia out the hospital room. *Shit, how did I fall asleep*, Patricia thinks on her way out.

"Aw, come on Patricia, you got to let me enjoy this just a little kiddo," Alisa proudly brags.

"You really need to be nice to me now, Patricia." Stopping in her tracks, Patricia turns to face Alisa.

"Why is that?" Patricia barks.

"Because, what's left of his life depends on a machine that is powered by a cord, that leads to a plug, and an electrical outlet. I decide if that plug gets pulled or not," Patricia is speechless. Stunned at Alisa's bravery. She flaunts her craziness so boldly and with so much pride. Heavily, Patricia sighs. She then begins to pace the hospital halls back and forth for a short moment. *This crazy bitch*, she thinks as Alisa watches her lose her cool. Patricia wants to blurt; *may God bless your soul* but everything in her gut tells her that Alisa could care less about God blessing her soul. So instead of blurting anything, Patricia angrily struts out the hospital. When she's finally in her car, she takes a minute to grab control of her emotions. She badly wants to break down in tears but her pride won't allow it.

The clicking of Patricia's heels echo throughout the halls. Speedily, she approaches *The Hawk's* front desk.

"Um, excuse me, I'm looking for…." Before Patricia can finish her sentence, Jason appears from behind a closed door.

"Oh, never mind, I see him," Patricia retorts before catching up to Jason.

"I've been calling you all night," Jason blurts before Patricia can get a word out.

"I need your help; I don't know anything about civil court," Patricia retorts, breathless. Her hair is unkempt and she looks like she feels, a mess. She hadn't been home since the trial and that much is obvious to Jason.

"I got to get a restraining order out on this woman or she's going to pull the plug on her husband." Jason is appalled, he thought for sure Patricia would have learned her lesson and been ready to put the horrid case behind her, but sure enough he was wrong.

"What is this, what are you doing, Patricia?" he leans in closer to her space and mumbles.

"What do you mean, what I'm I doing?" Patricia couldn't see what Jason was making so obvious. He wanted nothing to do with her and the case. As the partners of the firm and *The Hawk* himself appear from behind the same door Jason appeared from, Jason's body language gets stiff.

"You shouldn't be here," Jason murmurs before walking off to catch up with the other partners.

"I need contacts, like a family member, a close friend, something, anybody," Patricia responds.

"I really tried, Patricia. I really did but I can't help you."

"Aye, aye!" Patricia grabs Jason's arm and aggressively he jerks away.

"Don't!" he hisses through his clenched jaw.

"This woman is going to kill her husband; I need your help." Quickly, Patricia stops the doors on the elevator. Standing in between the doors, she pleads for Jason's help like a junkie pleading for crack cocaine.

"This woman is going to kill her husband," she repeats like a broken parrot.

"And what does that have to do with *The Hawk*?" The stiff white men, including *The Hawk,* burn a hole through Patricia's skin as they watch the elevator doors clos. It's beginning to be her most humiliating year.

In a rush back to her office, Patricia runs into Koch in the hall way. She nearly knocks him over trying to stop him. His security/driver quickly grabs hold of her arm the moment she touches Koch.

"It's okay, I got it," Koch says.

"Do you know any civil court judges?" Patricia blurts, following closely behind Koch who's on his way out the door.

"I just need a number," she continues between breaths. Barely keeping up with Koch's speed in the three-inch heels that are killing her feet.

"Have you been home at all today?" Koch finally stops and Patricia exhales short puffs as she tries to catch hold of her breath.

"No, I've been trying to find somebody who can put me in touch with a civil court judge."

"There is a restraining order out against you." Irritable, Patricia bends to her knees and then burst into laughter.

"I got a restraining order out against me?" she repeats in disbelief. "Oh, I don't even believe this shit," she muffles.

"You were at the hospital, right? Overnight." Patricia continues to giggle.

"And that warrants her to put a restraining order out against me?"

"Yes," Koch answers.

"She has a lawyer now. They went to Judge Brown this morning."

"Hold up for a second, who is her lawyer?" Patricia questions.

"It doesn't matter. Listen to yourself. You need to start looking out for yourself. She can have you arrested."

"You had one shot," Koch reminds Patricia.

"I know I had one shot, and I blew it, alright."

"She walked, and there's nothing we can do. She is a private citizen now; we have no standing. When you are done, you are done. Those are the rules."

"But, what about him?"
"You have to worry about yourself now," Koch answers firmly.

"Naw, I've done that. I've done a lot of that actually," Patricia answers with her head down looking more pitiful than a sad puppy.

"Go home and get some rest. It's over." Koch adds before disappearing into passing crowd.

CHAPTER 23

Patricia pulls the heavy Persian rug towards the hallway and off the wall-to-wall carpeting. Grabbing the vacuum cleaner and wrapping the thin cord around her smooth brown hand, she turns the power on and begins the task of cleaning the carpet. Humming an old Betty Wright tune, she pushes and pulls the vacuum until beads of sweat form above her nut-brown upper lip. Whenever Patricia has a lot on her mind, she cleans. Cleaning is her meditation; it helps her sort out her thoughts.

Alisa's revenge on her husband has burned a lot of innocent by-standers. She has not only ruined Patricia's career, but her relationship as well. In just a matter of weeks, Patricia's life has demoted from sugar to shit. The thought sends burning chills up Patricia's spine and she turns off the vacuum to grab her glass that's filled to the rim with Hennessey and Coke. "I'll be damn if I let this rich bitch ruin what I got going on. Unlike her, I need my damn job," Patricia murmurs before taking another sip of the Hennessey.

Alisa is well off. She didn't have to clock in to get her bills paid. She owns a multimillion dollar real estate company, plus she's a celebrity chief. Money for her is good. Patricia, on the other hand, has a boss. She must follow orders to keep her earnings coming in. Her brain is a thought away from exploding as she tries to think of a legal way to stop Alisa from killing her only hope to victory; Alisa husband. With Dawson dead, there will be no way she can stop Alisa. She will walk free, getting away with attempted murder. Shot after shot, Patricia gets wasted. Alcohol for Patricia during her most vulnerable moments is always a bad idea. She gets emotional and horny. It never fails. She badly wants to call Jason but dares not. He earned himself the silent treatment for weeks after the way he treated her at the firm.

Tired from cleaning, Patricia props up on the couch with her legs up, sipping on the Hennessey and Coke, humming to Betty Wright. Patiently, she waits for her chicken breasts and baked potatoes to finish baking. The loud ringing phone breaks Patricia's gaze. She figures it must be someone from work or Jason calling from an unknown number. She picks it up and says,

"Hello." The man on the other end of the line answers,

"Hello, may I please speak to Tracey."

"I'm sorry, you have the wrong number."

"Is this 555-2139?" he asks.

"No, this is 555-1239."

"Sorry, my mistake. Have a good evening!"

"You do the same." Hesitantly, Patricia hangs up the phone. She is so lonely that she yearns for conversation, attention, love from anybody. With Jason acting new and everything at work going left, she needs some sort of pillow. Some sort of distraction to take her mind off her shitty problems.

She pops up from the sofa frantically, when she realizes she forgot about the chicken in the oven. She rushes to the kitchen to take out the chicken and then she throws a pouch of boil-in the-bag rice into a pot on the stove when the phone rings again. Patricia assumes the same thing she did the first time, must be Jason or somebody from work. Wrong again, because the unknown man called Patricia back. Unintentionally, Patricia ends up flirting with him on the phone for over an hour. He has a deep, mesmerizing, sexy-ass voice, and Patricia is super turned on.

She tells him her name is Candice because it sounds sexy. He tells her his name is Morris for the same reasons. In little to no time, he makes Patricia feel comfortable and at ease. She isn't sure if he's a good finesser or if she's just lonely as hell. Either way, she's enjoying the attention. On her sofa, she sits, sipping Hennessey and Coke, kicking shit with a stranger on the phone. Talking about everything under the sun. From the latest Puff Daddy and family CD, to their respective careers, to her hair appointments the next day. For an hour, Patricia didn't have any worries. She didn't think about her problems not once.

Even though the conversation is stimulating, she finally tells him she must go because it's getting late and she needs to rest up. Patricia doesn't know where tomorrow is going to take her with this unresolved problem with Alisa she has dangling over her head. He asks her if he could call again sometimes and she replies, "No, that wouldn't be a good idea." For all she knows, he could be a killer, a robber, or worse, somebody Alisa sent her way. Conversation with him was good but she was smart enough to keep things blank about her real personal life. Even though, she didn't get a creep vibe form him. In a way, she feels God sent him to her to rebuild her strength. She no longer wants to break down anymore. Her emotions are under control, but her hormones, well that's another story.

CHAPTER 24

David: Do you know this psycho bitch is pulling the plug on her husband today?

The howl of Patricia's cell phone broke her sleep. "Fuck!" Patricia shrieks when she opens her eyes and looks around her bedroom. Spinning in circles, her head feels like someone is playing drums on her cranium and she can't move. She tries to lift but she falls flat on her back. The aching in her skull is the worse feeling ever. Now she understands why they call it a hangover; it feels as if the blackest of clouds is dangling over her head with no intention of clearing until late afternoon.

After three attempts, Patricia finally find the strength to lift her body up from the bed. She grabs her phone and reads David's text with her eyes squinting. Her mouth is dry, sticky with thick saliva.

"Shit!" she screams after reading the text.

"That fucking bitch!" As quick as she can, Patricia wobbles to the restroom. She splashes cold water on her face just to feel something refreshing. Instantly, she wishes she could wash her brain free of the toxins too. The mirror shows her eyes, she's no longer the glamour girl out of a magazine.

"I don't have time for pretty today," she mumbles as she washes her face and brushes her teeth. She speed-dials David but there is no answer. Without taking a shower, she slips on a suit she wore earlier this week. In less than ten minutes, she arrives at Jason's mother's house. Debbie is her only hope. Swiftly, Patricia struts up to the house and barges in without warning. The Judge is sitting mannequin like at the dining room table sipping on hot tea.

"I have nowhere else to go," Patricia blurts as soon as she locks her eyes on Debbie.

"I need your help. She's going to kill her husband. I got to stop her, I got to!" Expressionless, the judge stares blankly at Patricia and then slides her the court order. Stunned, Patricia hesitantly grabs the paper. *It's no way Debbie is that cool*, she thinks before looking down at the paper.

"A court order! Thank you. How did you know?" Patricia blurts.

"A good judge knows these things. Now, I don't know if it'll hold up in appeal," Judge Debbie answers calmly.

"No, that's okay. I just have to stop her. This will do! Thank you, thank you!" Patricia screams on her way out the door.

"Hold that elevator for me please!" A second too late, Patricia misses the elevator. So, she decides to take the stairs.

"Aye, aye!" she yells pounding on the glass window at Alisa and the nurse. Patricia is wheezing from the stairs and her chest is heaving up and down as if she's been chased by a dog.

Alisa cuts her eyes at Patricia. If looks could kill, Patricia would be dead already.

"Turn off the ventilator," the doctor demands.

"Aye stop!" Patricia yells banging on the room door. The doctors and nurses don't bother looking out at Patricia. They are standing around Dawson like he's lying in a casket at his viewing. There are tons of flowers decorating room. Alisa went all out; flowers, bears, and cards.

"I have a court order; you must stop this now!" Patricia shrieks. Three more beats and the hospital security jumps up from his seat.

"Ma'am this is a hospital. You cannot beat on the doors. I'm going to have to ask you to leave." Swiftly, Patricia marches towards the security.

"Listen here you rental cop, I got a court order. She cannot do this. You must let me in there," Patricia scuffles with the security to get to the room but she is outweighed. Out the corner of her eyes she can see more security charging towards her.

"Step outside for me ma'am, please."

"I got a court order; she repeats like a mocking bird."

"Ma'am, please leave before we arrest you." The second security officer adds. And without warning, Patricia breaks down. The tears burst forth like water from a dam, spilling down her face. She can feel the muscles of her chin tremble like a small child, and then she looks towards the window and there is Alisa, grinning like everything is funny. Life's nothing more than a game to her and Patricia is sadly losing. The banging in Patricia head occurs once more and she isn't sure if it's a side effect from the drinking or the constant stress she's been living with. Salty drops fall from her chin, drenching her gray wool blazer.

"Pull it together Patricia, pull it together." The crying worsens and she cannot stop it. *Dammit, why I can't I pull it together? Why can't I stop crying,* Patricia thinks as she continues to whimper on the outside. After sixty long seconds of that, Patricia finally makes her way onto the elevator. If she had any dignity left, she had lost it all in that moment.

The bar is a standing room, the smoke is thick and the music is loud. Loud enough to drown out all of Patricia problems. Singing the blues classics, by sisters like Ms. Holiday, comes extremely easy for Patricia. The blues got her acholic mother through her roughest times. She would play her music loud and sing along as she wept in her sorrow. Mirror to her mother, Patricia finds herself in the position ten odd years later.

As she begins to sing *Good Morning Heartache,* she thinks about how drastically her life had changed over the month. Sipping on the same Hennessey and Coke that had her spinning earlier, Patricia gets wasted.

She glances over at the piano player and instantly, every hormone in her drips into her panties. While the people in the audience are applauding and whistling at the band, she's giving the pianist one sexy ass stare. She can see the passion from his soul escape through his fingertips, onto the piano, and it's a pure turn-on. She begins to fantasize about how it would be if they made love, what his passionate fingers would feel like all over her body. Would he play her body with the same intensity as he played the piano? Would he make her forget all her problems?

When he finishes his final song, a little after twelve, he approaches Patricia with the intention of simply carrying a conversation, but Patricia is so damn horny for him, she couldn't take talking to him. So, she dashes outside to catch a cab without even taking the time to tell the man why she was leaving in such a rush. She knew he was probably wondering what made her leave in such a rush, but she had never fantasied about a man the way she did watching him on stage. She badly wanted to rub her nipples and finger herself, but she sure as hell wasn't going to do it in front of a crowd of people.

However, doing it in a cab was a totally different matter. The driver, a foreigner who could barely understand her destination when she told him, almost wrecked when he notices why her fingers were tucked under her bag. She masturbated in the backseat, right then, and there. She knows it's raunchy, but she had to do it. She couldn't wait until she arrived at Jason's house. Tonight, she's going to use that spare key, she never uses.

CHAPTER 25

"**W**hat the fuck?" Patricia stands stiff as a mannequin in the middle of Jason's seating area with her mouth drooped open. Her heart is racing like a running horse. Her eyes in disbelief. The neighbor from across the street's face is covered with Jason babies. His dick is dangling in front of her like a running fountain.

"You motha-fucka!" Patricia blurts out.

"How dare you?" she yells.

"Patricia, calm down. You know we are on a break," he replies as he tucks his penis back into his pants.

"A break?" she questions.

"Yes, a break." The thin brunette pops up from the floor and dashes to the hall bathroom.

"Naw, don't run now, bitch! And isn't that hoe married with kids?" Patricia shrieks.

"I don't know. That's none of my or your business."

"You fucking know nigga. Don't play stupid. I ought to go over there and tell her husband what she's over here doing." Like a track star, the brunette runs from the restroom and pleads out,

"Please don't do that. I'm begging you please."

"Patricia, you're acting real ghetto right now. Real fucking ghetto." The nerve of this nigga, Patricia ponders before taking a swing at his face.

"Okay. Take it easy, Patricia. Don't blow a gasket. You got a good punch in, and I hope it makes you feel better." Patricia just rolls her eyes at Jason.

"Just go home for now to give yourself time to cool off."

"I don't need to cool off. You've made our status crystal clear, Jason."

"And so have you."

"And how is that, Jason? Because I took on a damn case at work?" she snaps.

"I stuck my neck out for you and you let me down."

"Yeah, but I'm not one in here getting my dick sucked by some white whore." This time Patricia grabs a paperback off the coffee table *The Swirl* by Cornelia Smith, and throws it at him, but he's quick and dodges it.

"You're pissing me off!" Jason is the sexiest when he is angry. His muscles are protruding out his white-tee and the snake like veins in his neck are giving off a bad boy vibe.

"Just go Patricia, you're acting like a child. Go cool off and come talk to me when you're in your right state of mind."

"So this is how we end, like a boxing match?" There is a crack in Patricia's voice.

"You're the one who started," he replies, mirroring a seven-year-old.

"You're a cold hearted bastard, you know that?" Patricia murmurs, trying her hardest to fight back tears.

"I'm sorry you feel this way, Patricia."

"I'm sorry I do, too." She walks over towards him, but this time he just stands there. She looks up at him and he cannot look back. She looks down at his feet and then pushes him towards the door leading to the garage. Touching him just burns.

"Where are my things?" she questions him.

"You can get it while I'm at work and please leave the key on the table." Patricia didn't have any more than three outfits and maybe a toothbrush to get, but she's run out of tactics.

"Leave the key on the table?" Patricia repeats.

"Don't, I don't care. Keep it. I'm going to change the locks anyway." The neighbor stands silently to the side with wet eyes. She's starting to feel guilty. She never meant to break up a happy home. She just wanted to get a piece of Jason's Mandingo.

"You don't have to change your locks baby, here's your key. I'm no burglar." Aggressively, Patricia tosses the key to his chest. Now his black eyes are glistening.

"I'm really, really sorry, Patricia."

"No you're not," Patricia snaps before slamming the door behind her. She turn the knob so hard she breaks two nails. Quickly, she runs to the car before a tear can drop. She sits back into the leather seats and before she can get one thought in, she can feel it coming; heartache. That thud. The acid tears. The tear inside her chest. Her stomach balled up in a knot. Finally, she lets out the biggest cry ever and then stopping for big long pauses. Her heart is breaking into a thousand pieces and she's not sure how she'll repair it. Before Jason or his little tramp comes to the door, Patricia scurs out the parking lot.

Not long after Patricia gets out the shower, she hears someone knocking at the front door. She does not rush to answer it. For starters, she has a doorbell, and second, there's a sign out front that says as plain as day in English, Spanish, and giant red letters, *NO SOLICITORS*.

Crying the night before did Patricia some good. Her soul feels clean and her attitude is back on *Fuck You*. Like every other hard time in her life, she's determined to get over it. She had thought Jason was the one for her, just like she assumed working for *The Hawk* was the best thing smoking. But clearly, she was wrong, like when she assumed Alisa was a joke.

She puts on a pair of shorts, and while pulling the tank top over her head, Patricia can't believe it when she starts crying. She assumed she got it all out last night. The person at the front door is now knocking hard, entirely too hard for any solicitor. She wipes her eyes and runs down the stairs. Patricia is surprised to see Koch through the peephole. He has a worried look on his face. This is the second time he's dropped by her place and he didn't just pop-up for nothing, so she knows something is wrong. She opens the door.

"Patricia, are you okay? I've been standing out here forever but I saw your car in the garage and figured maybe you just didn't hear me. Can I come in?" she steps away from the door and opens it wide enough for him to enter.

"Do you want me to help you with that?" Koch takes the handkerchief from his pressed black suit and hands it to Patricia. One look in her eyes and he can tell she's been crying.

"So what now?" he asks as she dabs her wet eyes.

"Not this," she responds. "I'm going to try out something else, I'm getting out of law."

"You belong in a prosecutor's office," Koch responds.

"What are you going to do? Get fired just to rehire me?" Patricia flops down onto the sofa.

"It's still my office, at least until next election."

"Thank you but no thank you," she replies.

"We all lose, Patricia." Koch takes the picture from the mantle and then takes a long look at the picture of Patricia posing by a short slim tree that's starving for Christmas gifts. He knew for a black woman to accomplish what she'd accomplished, she really had to work for it.

"I let a woman get away with murder. How am I supposed to live with that?"

"You learn to," Koch answers placing the picture back onto the mantle and then turning to give Patricia his undivided attention.

"Well, I hope not." Speechless, Koch walks over to Patricia and offers her the warmest hug. The old white man inhales her dove and Enchanted Bath and Body Works lotion. Thinking, good gracious, this woman smells heavenly. It's clear, Patricia isn't feeling up to herself at the moment and he knew there was nothing he can say at that very moment to change that.

"Oh, you know if it makes you feel any better, technically you let a woman get away with attempted murder," Koch says on his way out the door.

"Don't beat yourself up about it," he adds before closing the door behind him.

CHAPTER 26

O kay, so, Cat Woman," Jamellah whispers to Patricia.

"You cannot be serious," Patricia replies loudly, and then takes a sip from the second bottle of water she's had in less than the hour they've been at the park. She's super dehydrated. LA heat has her drained.

She and her childhood friend Jamellah take a yoga class. Well, they're not exactly participating, they're standing far back by the trees, away from the crowd. Watching as the teacher teaches the paying participants. Patricia wanted to do a stress reliever exercise but Jamellah wasn't down for paying for some yoga class.

"Shit, I can teach my own self how to be quiet and stretch," Jamellah said when Patricia suggested the idea.

"There is no way in hell I can get my body to do any of these movements."

"They're called poses, Patricia."

"Whatever. And why aren't there any black people in there?" Patricia replies.

"I don't know. Just be quiet and watch," Jamellah answers. Maybe ten seconds pass.

"Did you really have to bring them damn annoying dogs?" Patricia breaks the silence to ask.

"Are they making noise? No, they are not." Rocki and Chanel are chillin in their carrier. Patricia rolls her eyes and then takes her attention off the yoga crowd.

"So how long have you been doing this online dating stuff?" Patricia asks Jamellah.

"Why?" Jamellah snaps.

"Because you haven't mentioned it to anybody, that's why. Are you embarrassed about it?" Patricia sips more of her water.

"No! Why would I be embarrassed? I told you, didn't I?"

"You usually tell me all of your personal business, that's why."

"Well, I took a page out of Patricia Patterson's book. I stopped telling all of my personal business."

"I tell you everything. Don't do that," Patricia barks.

"You mean everything, like this case that's all over the television?" Patricia called Jamellah up to get away from her problems, not talk about them, but she knew the conversation would come up eventually.

"That's different. That's business, you know I can't talk about that with you." Jamellah toots her lips up and mumbles,

"Umm, if you say so."

"I can't. I will say that this bitch is crazy."

"I know, that's all they've been talking about in the shop, girl."

"Why do you play the news in your shop anyway? You should be able to go get your hair done in a calming environment," Patricia adds.

"Girl, it's the customers who demand I turn the news on. So, do you think she really killed him?" Shaking her head in amusement, Patricia answers,

"Girl, what did I just tell you?"

"What? Nobody is looking, tell me. I'm just asking your opinion," Jamellah whispers.

"Hell yeah, I think she did it. I just can't fucking prove it," Patricia   mumbles.

"Oh she good, if you can't take her down. She's must be really good. I just knew you were going to demolish her ass." Shameful, Patricia murmurs,

"Yeah, she's good."

"I hear he used to cheat on her a lot. I think he was something like a jig-a-low," Jamellah adds.

"Anyway, enough about the case I told you I can't talk about, and a little more about this dating thing you got going on." It's far more to the Alisa case than Jamellah would ever know. Patricia's pride and ego wouldn't allow her to tell Jamellah how much she's lost dealing with this case.

"Anyway, I wanted to wait until I met somebody nice, that's why I haven't filled you in. Plus, I didn't want you dogging me and making me feel desperate."

In the back of Patricia's mind, she's thinking, *Hell, I'm the one who's desperate.*

"But you are desperate, aren't you?" Patricia jokes.

"Yeah, but so is half of LA," Jamellah kids.

"How long have you've been signed up?"

"About a month now."

"Do you really think you're going to meet somebody on an online dating service who's worth getting serious about?" Patricia wants to know for her own purposes, but it comes off like she's judging.

"There you go. Hell, why not give it a chance? I've tried everything else," Jamellah replies.

"Like what?" Patricia crosses her arms, waiting for Jamellah to come up with a decent lie.

"Okay, so, I'm a little dated. But, you've been out of circulation for years, Patricia."

Well, I'm back in now, Patricia thinks.

"You know people don't actually go to happy hour no more." Both Patricia and Jamellah burst into laughter at the joke.

"Do you know anybody that's had any luck doing this?" Patricia's curiosity becomes suspicious to Jamellah and she responds,

"You sure want to know a lot about this crazy online dating? Is everything good in paradise?" Smoothly, Patricia ignores the million-dollar question.

"No seriously, I just want to know," Patricia responds.

"No, I don't know anyone personally, but I've read a lot of testimonials." And just like that, Patricia has steered Jamellah's attention into the original direction. She's so easy to distract.

"You can certainly rely on those," Patricia sarcastically responds.

"You know what, Patricia? I'm looking at this whole thing like I do when I'm shopping and trying to find the perfect nude pump or the perfect red dress. You have to try on different ones and walk around in them until you find one that fit.," Patricia giggles and then shakes her head.

"Whatever, I'm about tired of this yoga crap. Let's go."

"How are you tired when we didn't even participate?" The girls giggle again. It's the most laughing Patricia has done all month. She knew getting up with Jamellah would help some. They were always good together. Since high school they've been like peanut butter and jelly. Jamellah was the only person Patricia knew that wanted something else out of life than what Compton had to offer.

They roll up the mats they had laid out on the grass. Looking at them, you'd swear they were about to work out. Patricia is wearing a purple-and-white getup that complements her curves all too well. Jamellah on the other hand, is far from curvy. She's all legs and bones. She has no boobs and her ass is flatter than a white girl on a diet. Patricia thinks she can really afford to gain a few pounds but she wouldn't dare tell her that.

"Well chick, as usual, I enjoyed your company. Don't let it be twelve years and another lost case before I see you again." Jamellah's hug is warm and comforting. She wraps Patricia's full body up in her little arms and then plants a small kiss on her forehead.

"This woman had to be planning this murder for months. Don't beat yourself up about it. She was bound to beat whoever took on the case." Jamellah blurts out on her way to her car.

"Who said I was worried about it?" Patricia blurts back.

"I know you like my favorite TV show, girl." Patricia's smiles wraps from one ear to another. She couldn't argue with that, Jamellah has always had her figured out. For a couple of hours, Patricia felt warm inside again and for a couple of hours, Patricia was a bad ass diva again.

CHAPTER 27

What Achton remembered about the day he lost Monroe is falling. First to the floor. Then being picked up by his daughter. He remembers the news saying something about Monroe taking her own life. With her own gun. One shot to the head. Right in the middle of the courtroom. He melted. Then his body stiffened and froze. His teeth would not stop chattering. He bit his tongue trying to silence them. He went looking for his car keys, he figured Monroe would want to tell him person what happened at court like she would do anytime she was dealing with a big public case.

"Where did I put them fucking keys?" he asked Chelsey as he walked from one room to the next, looking for them. They were, of course, in the same spot they always were; hanging on a hook by the door that led to the carport. Chelsey just shook her head. She tried her hardest to keep it together for her daddy, who was clearly losing his mind. Chelsey grabbed Achton by the wrists, then wrapped her arms around her father as tight as she could.

"Daddy," Chelsey said, bending over pulling him close and with a firmness that made it hard for him to move.

"You don't need your keys."

"But I should go get your mother, she's probably taking this case hard!" he screamed, wiggling his way out of her grip.

"Dad, you've gotta calm down." Achton looked at Chelsey like she was crazy, for a minute he forgot she was his daughter, who too had just lost her mother.

"Come on, you can go with me. I think she is going to be surprised to see us. We can pick up her favorite, pizza and salad. I probably need to take a shower. I stink, I've been working out. I'm filthy. Can you give me a minute or ten? I need to take a shower. Maybe, you should call her and let her know we're coming so she doesn't leave. Where's my cell phone?"

"Dad, you got to stop," Chelsey sighed. That's when Achton remembered Chelsey breaking down and drooping as if she didn't have a muscle in her body. She folded her arms on the kitchen counter and her head drooped on top of them. Achton heard her wail, then whimper. He wanted to hold her; for her to feel less pain than he was feeling, but he had collapsed on the sofa and could not get up. He crossed his arms but they broke apart and fell into his lap. Achton forced himself to blink enough to see through the tears and then pushed himself to the edge of the cushion and sat up straight.

He closed his eyes and himself; balancing. He was thinking that if he sat still long enough, maybe he could rewind this movie to the night before, when he and Monroe watched *Beaches* and cried like babies on the same sofa he sitting mourning her death.

Reality is setting in and Monroe's death isn't a bad dream. Achton casts his eyes to the freshly dug soil. Monroe is down there and God has taken her. *What the hell did he need her for?* he thought. The priest says he "Called her home" with a dopey look on his smug little face. Achton imagines his features rearranged by the business end of a shovel. She already had a God damn home and damn God for taking her.

When he gets to heaven he's kicking his ghostly ass all around the God damn place and burning the pearly gates. All that is left now is Chelsey with her half-ass Daddy. A daddy who doesn't even know how to break a smile or utter a kindness. A daddy who finds fault in every God damn little thing and uses his meaty hands like the raw hunks of meat they are. God took the wrong damn parent!

"Damn you God!" he kicks at the soil, feeling the only love he'd ever known drain right through his boots and be replaced by ice.

"Momma! Noooo, don't leave me!" Chelsey utters the most hysterical crying; the screaming sobs only interrupted by her need to draw breath. It's a primal sound, one we're programmed not to ignore. Gently, Patricia wraps her hand around Chelsey's and pulls her in close to her.

"Let it out baby girl, let it out," she murmurs to her.

"Please, please God!" Chelsey pleads out with her head held up to the sky, where God is said to cohabitate. Speechless, Patricia smoothly breaks away from the bond with Chelsey. She tries to slip away through the crowd but before she gets far Chelsey whimpers out, "Please get who's responsible for this. Please make them pay!" Uttering no reply, Patricia pulls her dark shades down over her eyes and walks away.

CHAPTER 28

"**H**ello?" Patricia answers irritably.

"Hey," Jason's voice says softly on the car phone.

"Hey," Patricia answers, feeling helpless. Relieved that she is not being hostile, Jason contemplates on his next move. Breathing deeply, he decides to lay his cards on the table.

"Pat, I'm sorry. I know that may never be enough, but I need you to know that. Pat, we need to talk. Can I come and get you?"

"Yes," is the only answer that Patricia can muster up. She thinks about going haywire on him but she doesn't have the energy, plus she's interested in what he has to say.

"Are you home?"

"Yes." Patricia's reply is drier than a desert.

"I'm on my way." Jason cannot afford Patricia changing her mind, so he ends the calls as soon as he finishes his sentence.

Patricia sits in her car in her driveway. She's still in her suit from the funeral. Her eyes are tucked behind her famous Sinatra style shades. The radio plays softly in the back ground, mellowing out Patricia and calming her rattled nerves. Ten minutes after she dozes off, she hears a soft tap on her window. Opening her eyes, she sees Jason crouching down next to her car window looking at her. Switching off the ignition, she puts the keys in her jacket pocket and opens the door. Stepping out, looking like a mourning widow, she stands next to Jason silently, refusing to say one word.

It was Jason who messed up, it's Jason who's going to have to clean up.

"Wanna take a ride?" Jason asks uncertainly. He knew going into her house after what he has done is not an option. Nodding, Patricia follows him while he walks to his Benz and unlocks the door. Getting in on the driver's side, he opens the door and urges her in. Once she settles, he pushes down the lock and shuts the door. Getting in on the driver's side, he starts the engine. After driving around silently and aimlessly for the better part of an hour, Jason speaks up.

"I've miss you, Pat. I miss our good times. It's harder than I thought it would be not having you around." He waits to hear a response. After hearing her sigh softly, he knows what he must do; beg.

"Pat, baby, I am sorry for what I did. There is not a minute or an hour that I don't think about it. I can only imagine how you must feel. I never meant to break your heart; you have to believe me." Hearing her let out a rush of air, he turns to see her shoulders trembling. Crying is one thing Pat can't seem to control these days.

Her outpour of emotions soon causes warm, salty tears to slip down Jason's face. Pulling over into an empty lot, he cuts off the engine and has himself a good cleansing cry.

The squeal of Patricia's phone breaks her sleep. She is shocked as hell to see that they have fallen asleep in the empty parking lot.

"Hello," she says breathlessly, answering the phone so Jason wouldn't be bothered.

"I got Monroe's folder when you're ready to look at it," David says.

"I'm on my way." Patricia ends the call and then turns towards Jason. He's quietly sleeping with dried-up tears on his face. Reaching out slowly, she intends to wake him up. She finds that she isn't able to bring herself to touch him. Instead, she decides a verbal awakening will work better.

"Jason? Jason," she pauses for a few seconds, surprised at the tenderness in her own voice. Making it a point to sound gruffer, she barks out his name. "Jason!"

"Huh?" Jumping, Jason wakes up and looks at her wildly with bloodshot eyes. Without waiting for her to answer, he smiles sheepishly and starts the engine.

"Where to Miss Daisy?" he jokes.

"Actually, I need to go to the office." Jason almost snaps, *what for?* until he realizes he isn't all the way in yet. Patricia can tell from the look on his face, he wants to question her decision. She's just patiently waiting for him to, so she can give him the blues, but he never does.

Patricia sits at her desk in her office, researching on the internet. She's desperate to find a way to put Alisa behind.

"Why am I doing this? Just let it go, Pat," she mumbles. She slams the pen down on the desk, eases back into her chair, and places her hand on her head. Patricia sits in deep thought. He can't shake Alisa's smirk from the hospital. Patricia's lost her dignity, job, and almost her man because of Alisa and badly, she wants her pay. For everything: Dawson death and her new added stress. Patricia's been getting very little sleep since she met Alisa. Her wicked games have been fucking with her mind and she knows if she wants to get back to sleeping, she must nail Alisa.

Lately, anything that resembles Alisa or concerns Alisa becomes an exhausting experience. Constantly, Patricia searches her files, Monroe's files, her law books, and the net; trying to figure out where things went wrong. She remembers Alisa's story about everything having a flaw and she just knows; Alisa's perfect murder isn't an exception. *If you look close enough, you'll find that everything has a flaw-a weak spot.* Alisa's words echo constantly in Patricia's head as she continues to sit at her desk, rocking back and forth in the comfy leather chair.

She looks down at the crumbled pieces of paper on the floor. There are five pieces balled up, representing all the dead ends she's run into. Hour after hour and still Patricia has nothing new. Nothing has changed, no new evidence, no new witnesses, no new nothing.

Night has come around again too soon. Pat rests her head on the cool glass desk.

The lights of the sunset creep in through the open blinds, painting the high ceiling a rusty gray.

Patricia stands up and stretches for the stars while yawning like a tired toddler. Her hand then ferrets arounds in her pocket for the 5-Hour Energy drink. She doesn't plan to drink it all, just half to keep her from falling asleep.

Alarmed, Patricia grabs her cell phone that is vibrating across the desk and looks at the caller I.D. with wide eyes. The number is unknown. Patricia answers the call but says nothing.

Her heavy breathing is the only confirmation that she is on the phone.

"Hello, kiddo." Instantly, Patricia's eyes glisten with fire. Just the sound of Alisa's voice boils her blood. Still, she is silent. She doesn't reply.

"I thought I should call you and let you know, I'm taking that vacation we talked about, although it will not be the same without our Dawson. I know you like to keep tabs on me, so I thought I should just let you know." Angrily, Patricia flips through Monroe's files. She's looking for nothing but her nerves are rattling and she needs a distraction.

"Anyway, I have a little something for you. It's a present. A little gift. I was going to send it to *The Hawk* but—umm, I guess that's not working out anymore." Like a Christmas miracles, suddenly a light bulb is turned on in Patricia's head as she flips through Monroe's files. It all made sense now.

David walks in just as Patricia discovers this new information and she lip-syncs to him, *this is Alisa on the phone, I got to go.* She then covers the bottom end of the phone and say aloud, "Get the boys and meet me at her house."

Are you crazy? Are you out your mind? David lip-sync's back with the ugliest facial expressions. Fearfully, he shakes his head, *no* and signals with his waving hands *stop.*

"Meet me there," Patricia whispers on her way out the door, covering the bottom end of the phone again.

"And the deeds office didn't have a forwarding address. Do you have any suggestions?" Alisa continues with her bragging. She knows work and winning is everything to Patricia, and now neither is working in her favor.

"How about, I just come and get my gift from you?" Patricia breaks her silence to say.

"Suit yourself kiddo," Alisa replies before ending the call.

CHAPTER 29

Patricia gets that feeling in her stomach again, the one she had the day of the trial. It's a soft mixture between nausea and electric tingles. Her head begins to buzz and her heart rate increases as if she's running away, like she wants to. Alisa's home lies ahead. Even though she's walking, it feels more like the driveway is a conveyor belt; like she's a cow in the slaughter house heading towards the captive bolt.

Alisa likes to intimidate while appearing to be professional. She's mastered the many ways to be professionally nice and ways to be professionally unpleasant. She is a champion at the game. She knows just what to say on record and off. She hardly makes mistakes, which makes Patricia even more nervous.

Silently, Patricia enters Alisa's house without a *knock* or a *hello*. Patiently, waiting for her arrival, Alisa sits in the dark watching her cameras. Closely, she watches as Patricia sneaks around her house on her tip toes. She's looking around as if she's in a museum shopping for art.

"Good even, Patricia."

Startled by Alisa's voice, quickly Patricia turns around. She locks eyes with Alisa who is sitting pretty in her Givenchy dress, sipping on her red wine at her dining table.

"I didn't know you liked art; I would have gotten you some," Alisa says, speaking of the art mounted on the wall Patricia was once staring at.

"But then, I don't think you deserve a gift since I didn't get a thank you for the first one."

"Sorry to disappoint you." Patricia takes a seat on the opposite end of the dining table. Silence vents for twenty-long seconds and then Alisa utters,

"It takes a very special sort of person to look into someone's eyes and shoot them, Patricia. It takes a certain kind of strength, if you know what I mean." Appalled yet again by Alisa's cockiness, Patricia sits with an amusing smile.

"Well, I guess you would know," Patricia replies with a smirk on her face.

"Oh, yes I would." Instantly, Alisa is rushed with flashes of the shooting. The sweet joy of watching him drop to the ground welcomes a smile on her face.

"Anyway, I've got another bag to pick up. Don't you start shooting without me, Patricia." Patricia grips on tight to the .45 she assumed Alisa didn't see in her blazar pocket. She gets up and follows Alisa down the foyer to the seating area.

"I noticed something," Patricia blurts.

"It's a little late. Oh hell, it's a lot late." Now that Patricia has Alisa's attention, she flops down onto the sofa. Curious, Alisa is attentive.

"I noticed, that-um you and-um-Monroe have the exact same gun." Playfully, Patricia spins Monroe's gun on her index finger.

"Yes, so?" Alisa snaps, unbothered by the Alisa's little discovery.

"That's why you went to the hotel that afternoon, isn't it? You took her gun and you simply swapped it with yours."

"I gave it back." Arrogant, Alisa giggles.

"Right, you gave it back the night of the arrest. You knew once Monroe saw Dawson she would be thrown off guard. All she could see was him. You knew she would just walk the murder weapon right out of the house, didn't you?" The sound of Alisa's clap echoes throughout the house.

"That's very cleaver, I must admit. I couldn't see that coming with binoculars," Patricia adds.

"It wasn't just cleaver, Patricia. It was beautiful. She sat through the entire trial wearing the only piece of evidence on her hip," Alisa brags.

"Yeah, and then she used it on herself. Do you have any remorse?" Patricia blurts.

"Aww, pity. Sometimes life gives us these little gifts, if you know what I mean?"

"I do know what you mean. I know exactly what you mean because I got the bullet. The one in your husband's head," Patricia replies calmly.

"Yeah, now you got your little bullet, don't you? You got what you want. So, bring it on kiddo. Bring it to court, except you can't, can you?" Alisa's smile mirrors a winning lottery inheritor.

"Let's see now, there's that law-double jeopardy. I went to trial, you lost. Boo-hoo, cry me a river. It doesn't matter what you do, it doesn't matter what you know. You see, he can come back from the dead and testify, spill the beans and it would mean nothing." Silently, Patricia sits with a smirk on her face, just listening to Alisa brag on her perfect murder.

"You can't touch me, ever." Again, Alisa giggles. This time her laugh last for a whole minute.

"You didn't let me finish. I got a bullet, the one in your husband's head. I'm pretty sure it's going to match Monroe's and that gives me a murder weapon." Alisa pauses in her trap and suddenly her smile is gone.

"Nicely done, Patricia. Nicely done," she claps before resuming her packing. Patricia gets up and follows her around like a little puppy.

"I bet you don't even need a confession anymore, do you, Pat? I tell you what kiddo. Let's make you a new one, detailing all the details. That'll make you happy won't it?" Patricia doesn't reply. She grips on tight to Monroe's gun as Alisa gets closer.

"I shot my husband in his face, right there," Alisa dents her dimple as she demonstrates.

"He didn't look so handsome, no more. I stood there looking down at him. I watched his eyes go all empty. I could smell the blood and the shit. It's smelled like metal. And the look on Monroe's face, oh my it was priceless," Alisa snickers. Patricia gawks her down like a hawk.

"She tried her hardest to get him back to life and I stood there laughing on the inside. You see, I took both of them bastards out with one, fucking, bullet. Yes." Proud, Alisa bursts into laughter again.

"He was alive," Patricia breaks her silence to say. Alisa stands puzzled at her response.

"When you first went to trial for attempted murder, your husband was still alive." The clicking of Patricia heels echoes throughout the house as she circles Alisa like she's prey.

"You just had to pull that plug, didn't you?" Alisa is no longer laughing but attentively listening with her eyes glued to Patricia's every movement.

"Well, now he's dead. That's murder, that's homicide first degree. That my friend is a new charges." Standing with her mouth drooped open, Alisa is for the first time tonight—silent.

"That's new evidence, that's a new trial." If this was baseball, fireworks would be popping right now. Patricia is back. She's won the game. The feeling is indescribable. She badly wants to show off her happiness but she keeps it cool, cute, and classic and only issues a half smile topped off with a smooth blink.

"Get the fuck out of my house," Alisa opens the door for Patricia and surprise. LAPD, is awaiting her arrival.

"I promise you'll regret not letting this go," she whispers into Patricia's ear before the police officer hauls her away.

"My word is my bond, kiddo!" she yells out as they tuck her head in the car.

UP NEXT!

(Available for Pre-Order)

NATIONAL BESTSELLING AUTHOR
CORNELIA SMITH

CHAPTER 1

"**T**urn around. Lift up your hair," the deputy says. Alisa has been booked for three hours, and after moving from a holding cell to the second floor, she's being forced to undress and stand under a freezing-cold shower. Choking on tears, she meekly lifts her hair up while the female deputy sprays an awful-smelling liquid onto her body.

"Why, couldn't this bitch just leave me alone?" Alisa manages to choke out. Being arrested is the most dehumanizing thing in the world, she thinks. She understands that she'd killed her husband, but didn't the fact that he cheated on her, broke her heart, and used her like a broom to sweep up the trash in his life count for anything?

"We need to make sure that you don't expose any of the inmates to any new strains of head or pubic lice. We have enough problems controlling the strains that we have here already," the deputy says kindly. *This woman doesn't look like she belongs in jail,* the rookie thinks. But then again, neither did half of the male and

149

female inmates. Handing Alisa a pair of shower slippers and an orange jumpsuit large enough to accommodate two people, she waits while Alisa dresses slowly and blindly through her tears.

Vaguely, Alisa hears the two-way radio on the deputies hip crackle. Watching as the woman walks away while talking into the radio, she takes a few minutes to try to compose herself. She feels like trash. Being treated like a common criminal. All for what, because a nosey DA couldn't let well enough be. *She will pay for this, if it's the last thing I do. On my dying bed, she will pay for this*, Alisa thinks as tears slowly roll down her cheeks.

"People of the state of California versus Alisa Hopkins." *Finally*, Alisa thinks as she rises from the mahogany bench.

"So, we meet again?" Judge Brown blurts out at Alisa.

"Unfortunately," Alisa murmurs back.

"Ms. Hopkins, you've been charged with section C-187-199 the California penal code for murder. Do you wave further reading of the complaint and complete statement of rights?" Softly, the Jewish lawyer whispers to Alisa,

"You do."

"I do," Alisa repeats after James Grier.

"And do you wish to enter a plea at this time?"

"I do," Alisa answers.

"How do you plea?" Judge Brown responds.

"Not Guilty, your honor." Before Patricia can chime in Grier blurts out,

"I'd like to file a motion to suppress, your honor."

"On what grounds?" Judge Brown questions.

"The confession taken by my client was Improperly obtained. She was heavy medicated on LSD. A drug prescribed by her doctor."

"Objection your honor, Ms. Hopkins was in a clear state of mind during her confession," Patricia blurts out.

"Your honor, my client's constitutional rights were violated. Ms. Patterson invited herself into my client's home, pretended to be her friend and coned a bogus confession out of her while she was heavily medicated," Grier snaps back.

"Motion granted; verbal confession will be thrown out." Patricia's Chinese cut bang blows upwards as she heavily exhales.

"Thank you, your honor," Grier replies.

"Ms. Patterson, I don't want this to turn into a repeat of the hideous nightmare we had before. Ms. Hopkins is a tax paying citizen and I want her to be treated as such. No hole, no leaks. Are we clear?" Judge Brown blurts out.

"Yes, we're clear." Patricia knows exactly where Judge Brown is going with his statement. He wants her on her toes and ready to play. He, like every other court official wants to see Alisa pay for her crime but he's also aware the entire state of California is following the case. So, every move must be made by the books.

Alisa sits at a table with her head down. A single hanging light shines down on her. District Attorney Patricia enters and sits in the chair directly across from her. She pulls a pack of cigarettes out, a lighter, and puts them on the table

"You need a smoke?" Patricia asks. Alisa shakes her head, *no.*

"To whom do I owe this pleasure?" Alisa jokes.

"Alisa I know your husband hurt you. In fact, he cut you deep. I'm a woman, I know that pain all too well," Patricia stares deep into Alisa's glistening eyes.

"I know you killed your husband and I understand why you did it. He played you like a video game. If you cooperate with me, I can make sure you don't do more than ten years in prison. You'll be on papers of course but you'll be free." Patricia believes the deal she's offering is a slam dunk and Alisa would be crazy to not take it. But, Alisa feels the complete opposite. Rudely, she burst into laughter. She isn't taking any deal. She will kill herself before she spent years in anybody's prison.

"I didn't kill my husband. Monroe, killed my husband." Stunned at Alisa's response, Patricia just shakes her head with disgust written all over her face.

"So, it that your plan? Are you kidding me right now?" Patricia replies.

"I don't have time for jokes kiddo, my life is on the line."

"And why on earth would she do that, huh? Why, would she kill your husband, Ms. Hopkins?"

"Because, he wouldn't leave me for her," Alisa replies calmly with no smirk or smile on her face.

"I don't have time for this." Patricia gathers up her manila folder and jumps up from the table.

"The deal is off, Ms. Hopkins. You had your chance," Patricia blurts on her way out.

www.ingramcontent.com/pod-product-compliance
Lightning Source LLC
Chambersburg PA
CBHW051831170626
46807CB00003B/1125